BOOKS BY **GRAYDON MILLER**

Hostages of Veracruz
The Havana Brotherhood
Mujeres con navajas
Watsonville Stories

THE HAVANA BROTHERHOOD

STORIES

Graydon Miller

GRADY MILLER BOOKS

THE HAVANA BROTHERHOOD

Author's photo by Don Goodman
(**ship2me@gmail.com**)

"International Bridge" was awarded the Political Short Story Prize by the University of Guadalajara.

"Rivals" first appeared in *El Informador;* "Poison Pen" first appeared in *Ellery Queen Mystery Magazine.*

ISBN 978-0986273421

Please contact the publisher at:
gradymillerbooks@gmail.com
1236 1/8 N. Cahuenga Blvd.
Hollywood, CA 90038

Contents

International Bridge

"If they stop us, they'll ask questions . . . They'll separate us to ask more questions and make us contradict ourselves . . . To divide us . . . We have to stick to a single story and never, ever betray it."

Aboard the swaying train, shuttling to the north, *el norte*, they fine tuned their plan. Outside the train window, the landscape changed: cornfields became maguey plantations and, beyond a sawtooth-edged range of blue mountains, grey veils were released by a distant summit—perhaps a volcano—and then everything dissolved into the long lunar agony of the desert. Neither Meche nor Evaristo paid a bit of attention to that spectacle of nature because so much depended on their plan, it dominated every thought.

They were going to cross the border, not disguised as oil drums or crouched in a truck with a false bottom.

They were going to cross the border, their heads held high, avoiding the humiliations of crawling in a rat-infested sewer, swimming across the filthy waters of the Río Grande or having to deal with a *coyote*. Evaristo and Meche were going to cross the border on foot, right under the nose of the *Migra*.

They ironed out details of the plan over and over, and Meche said yes to everything, but instead of paying attention to Evaristo, her mind strayed to a long-ago springtime in their land, where happy children frolicked by waterfalls and swam in a lake of water so crystal-clear the boats seemed to float in the air. She remembered the birdsong of the *zenzontle* and the jungle smells so clear after the rain, but the banshee-whistle of a falling bomb shattered the beautiful daydream. In reality, it was a locomotive whistle sounding, and Meche crouched down over Evaristo's knees. They heard some shouts issue from the cars ahead, and the whole train rocked with a tremendous shudder. During the dense silence that followed, Meche and Evaristo verified that they were still among the living; the train had come to an abrupt halt and a heavy cloud of dust enveloped everything.

"Wait, Meche. I'm going to look ahead to see what happened," Evaristo said.

He put his hands on Meche's shoulders and, before leaving the train car, and gave her an affectionate kiss on the nose. Meche waited in her seat, and while there was the clamor of men running along the side of the train tracks, she had to remind herself they had already left their war-torn country, and the bullets and bombs belonged to the past.

"A cow stopped on the tracks," said Evaristo, returning with a film of yellow dust on his shoulders. "Six men dragged it onto the side of the tracks. The worst of it is, the mother cow had a calf inside."

Lurching, the train started to move forward with new momentum, passing a group of people huddled around the wounded animal that still hadn't finished dying, the hooves still moved. Evaristo's hand brushed against Meche's long hair and squeezed her hand, as if to say, "Be not afraid. Everything will be fine."

Evaristo and Meche had met each other while escaping the terrible forces that had destroyed their families and threatened to destroy them. When the two refugees first met each other, they were mutilated inside, and then they seemed to form a complete being, a unique and indivisible orange, safe from the plague of war and its air infected with the taste of charred flesh and gunpowder. Toward the end of the last year, during the Christmas truce, they began to arduous trek to the north, thinking about the new life that was on its way. So many months of moving about, that is, if you can measure hell in months, meantime Meche's stomach was growing. Together they endured the hardships of the southern border of Mexico; they continued to suffer tribulations together and, afterward, little by little, they made enough money for the train tickets, and a little more, playing the guitar in city buses. Evaristo would sing in an enthusiastic out-of-tune voice, and

Meche would stumble around the moving buses and gather coins.

Now that they arrived at the border town, as twilight approached, it was possible to believe, if only for a moment, that everything was going to be fine.

As soon as their feet touched the train station pavement, they hurried off. Evaristo wanted to cross the border before the sun set: they would appear less suspicious before the pedestrian crowds thinned out. They went straight to a clothes store, where Evaristo lavished attention on his wardrobe, since it had to be authentic, as if they'd bought it on Whittier Boulevard or at Victor Clothing Company right on Broadway in Los Angeles. After buying flashy two-tone patent leather shoes, he chose of pair of chino pants that couldn't have been baggier and a wide Pendleton shirt that reached his knees, a blue bandanna and a rakish hat.

"How do I look?" he asked Meche.

She laughed, wondering whether they had any change left to buy a meal. Seeing the displeasure her response elicited, she quickly added, "You look like a real *pachuco*."

"One from the United States, ey?"

"Yes, Evaristo."

He was completely happy. Now that they had performed almost all the preparations for their plan, they couldn't back out. They had to be very alert to carry out every step of this derring-do, since the border sheriffs carried big pistols and had bloodhounds capable of sniffing out yesterday's trail. Yes. They had to be prepared.

Evaristo carried his battered guitar case festooned with stickers from different Mexican states they had traveled through—Chiapas and Veracruz and Chihuahua. American songs floated in the air perfumed with the fresh exhaust of cars stagnating on the threshold of the new country. A motley collection of people sold things with a rusty spiel rolling off their lips; Indian women sat cross-legged before their trinkets spread on threadbare serapes, their babies wrapped in shawls on their backs, while other children frolicked along the street, half undressed, their stomachs sticking out and seemingly happy. A legless man played the flute, the healthiest representative of a company of beggars, each more pathetic than the other, who competed for the charity of passers-by. Defying the speeding traffic, a pair of blind guitarists blundered along, the hand of one resting on the shoulder of one in front, creating an epidemic of screeching brakes, angry shouts, and horn honks.

Meche left Evaristo's side impetuously and extended her hand to one of the blind musicians, helping them reach the sidewalk, and she almost got run over herself.

"Meche, are you crazy?" Evaristo reprimanded. "Why did you do it? There was no reason to do that! We have to concentrate on our plan."

Meche strove to keep up with Evaristo's brisk pace, feeling the baby's movement in her body, but no longer being able to keep up the effort, she collapsed to her knees. Evaristo forgot about the guitar and helped her to stand up and, kneeling before her, he kissed the swollen belly and, brushing his cheek against it, spoke softly to the unborn child.

"You are going to be born in the United States. When you are big, you're going to be a great baseball player. Meche, don't worry, everything is going to be fine; soon we'll arrive, just a few more steps . . ."

"Yes, Evaristo. Yes, I'm fine."

But she wasn't. She felt something stronger stirring in her, but she didn't want to worry him with trivialities: they were about to cross the border. Holding hands, they crossed the concrete arch that led to the "pot of gold," the fortune and happiness that awaited them. A sweating mass of people milled around them: travelers, ne'er-do-wells, pick-pockets, preachers, and God knows who else, were crossing to the promised land. U.S.A. Three magical letters, the jingling of silver in the pockets and odd pieces of green paper.

"There we will have our own house and a bathroom with a shower. Our children will have shoes and will go to school," said Evaristo.

Now the other country was only a few feet away, and Meche and Evaristo went more slowly as if a gigantic invisible hand obstructed their progess. Both their hearts compressed and beat faster and faster, and Meche forgot her incipient labor pains amid the phantasmagoria of the strange place. She forgot about the life stirring within her.

"Do you feel different?" Evaristo asked, caressing

Meche's hair and looking deeply into her eyes.

"Why should I feel any different?"

"We're already in the U.S.A.," he said.

At the midpoint of the concrete span, they crossed a powerful, imaginary line that divides the two countries, and they still felt the same. As soon as Evaristo reminded her what she had to say to the immigration officers, they were caught up in a long line, which moved forward by fits and starts, and every time Evaristo, with the guitar in his hand, took Meche's arm and lifted the guitar case a few steps forward. These final moments of waiting became unbearable. A crown of sweat clung to Meche's scalp while a barefoot and dirty child, with circles around his eyes, tried to sell them chewing gum, the fever of hunger in his eyes, and a hand of skin and bone tugging at Meche's skirt. Ahead of them some college girls waited to re-enter their country, one of them making gum bubbles and wearing a huge Pancho Villa sombrero, while in the other line there were some drunken Marines, tall with crew cuts. Meche trembled from head to toes. Evaristo didn't have to ask, he already knew why: the sight of any military uniform, even though it belonged to Uncle Sam, reminded her of the butchers who massacred every member of her family and, quickly now, she sought refuge in the memory of the nights she and Evaristo passed, hugging each other, shivering in the bottom of a muddy ditch, as the war tanks rolled by, making the earth tremble.

Meche took her eyes from the Marines and, at that

instant, she felt a sudden chill. Evaristo had taken his arm away. She hadn't even realized that they had reached the head of the line, and Evaristo had already assumed the slouching stance of a *pachuco*, the shoulders lazy and drooping, the hips pushed forward; he had a bandanna down so low on his forward he could hardly see where he was stepping.

With an expression of exquisite boredom, Evaristo mumbled to the immigration officer in English learned from movies and songs.

"*Citizen American.*"

It appeared that this response did not satisfy the officer, because he was moving his mouth and looking at Evaristo suspiciously. A stream of words emerged that Evaristo couldn't have understood in a thousand years, with the aid of a hundred dictionaries. Clinging to the one trick in his slim repertoire, he repeated, this time with less aplomb:

"*Citizen American.*"

The immigration officer's brow wrinkled alarmingly. Evaristo's musical case had fallen open and the guitar slid out and hit the ground with a burst of dissonant chords. Meche said, hurriedly, while Evaristo leaned down and his hands fumbled for the guitar:

"*¡Apúrate, apúrate!*"

He rushed forward and, with a metallic sound that echoed for some time in Meche's hearing, he broke through the barrier of the turnstile's chrome arms. He was already there, in the country they had dreamt of for so long. She admired Evaristo so much! How much she loved the fearlessness of this skinny boy with an Adam's apple sticking out. She wanted to love him, bear his children and see him already on the afternoon of their golden wedding anniversary. Still immersed in her dream, Meche ran into the snout of an older, uniformed woman with watery eyes.

"*Aaaaaaeryamerikhn sddzzzzn?*"

Meche heard and the woman repeated it brusquely.

"Gringa," Meche stammered before the red nose and watery eyes and attempted to successfully play the role that Evaristo had assigned, and she was already more rattled by the guitar and the broken instrument case and the presence of the gum-selling child who returned to tug at her skirts. An embarrassing silence lengthened while Meche tried to order the words rehearsed a thousand times. Finally, they came out all in a jumble:

"We are brother and sister. We live Albuquerque. Our address is Yefferson Street," Meche added. "We are students of high school. We don't have I.D. card, it's because terrible wetbacks us rob."

"But, señorita . . ."

Meche's gaze searched desperately for Evaristo. He was smart, he'd think of something. She saw the plaid shoulders of Pendleton shirt and the blue bandanna recede. She shouted his name:

"Evaristo . . ."

Fool. She had completely forgotten the false name agreed upon beforehand.

"Señorita, move to one side, please," another immigration officer spoke. "Other people have to pass."

Evaristo had already taken three steps in the promised land and, like the man who senses a rifle scope on his back, he resisted turning his head, but behind him he could hear the strident voices and Meche's clumsy attempt to explain she was "gringa." And Meche, without being able to know how much Evaristo suffered at this moment, saw the blue bandanna glide among many heads and shoulders. He strode languidly as the tide formed, pouring more and more waves into the sea of people, and the echoes resounded on a cold shore of concrete. A third officer shouted something that hurt Meche's ear, and on a sudden impulse, she made way into the sea of people with thrusts of her arms. Hearing her awful shouts, Evaristo couldn't take it any more and risked a glance behind. Meche was moving her arms like machetes and babbling incoherencies. He didn't want to leave her like that—"Don't leave her," a voice shouted inside Evaristo—he would have to stay behind and help her, but the brown and cream patent leather shoes continued moving ahead. "Don't leave me, don't leave me," a tiny voice clamored inside, but Evaristo did not stop, not then, not ever, and something died inside him.

"Evaristo . . . Evaristo!"

Meche left the guitar, lurched ahead and ran toward the blue bandanna that bobbed among many heads and shoulders. She touched his shoulder and a bug-eyed man with skin black as coal glared at her. Meche became queasy and fell to her knees, feeling a strong movement of little feet within her, as if Evaristo were trampling her own heart. She gave a soul-rending cry: the moment to give birth had arrived . . .

Meche spent a day and a half in the captivity of the *corralón* with a bed of concrete and anti-American curses scrawled on the cinderblock walls. Afterward, the Americans were going to transfer her and twenty others, crowded into a suffocating van, back to the Mexican authorities to do the rest of their time. What would happen when they realized Meche was a refugee from another country? There would be other scenes to act, risks to take, and roles to play. Fortunately, one of the officials of the *Migra* took pity on Meche, her extreme youth, and in view of what had befallen her the other night: a cold mass of flesh and gristle had been born to her, strangled by the same chord that had given it life. The official let her get off on a streetcorner of the border town.

"Don't come back, OK?" he said in a sad yet joking tone.

Meche raised the guitar case off the sidewalk and continued as if hypnotized, wrung out, without a fixed course. At nightfall, she reached an ugly place that was very difficult to remember after the trials of the last two days: the international bridge. No longer did people push and shove on either side, elbowing and shouting, fighting for the passing tourists' coins; the Indian women covered in *rebozos* and with babies on their backs had gone. There only remained the legless flute player.

In this dead and abandoned zone, Meche kneeled down. She and Evaristo had suffered so much together, loved so much during the nights when they covered each other with their sleeping bodies in ditches. And when the final test came, Evaristo had gone on without her. So be it. In spite of her stoic philosophy of "so be it" engendered by the war, Meche wept. She wept to the last teardrop . . . Lifting her tear-tarnished gaze, she saw a disheveled figure emerge from the darkness—one of the blind guitarists, who came alone, carrying the strings and wood of a smashed guitar.

"Ay, señorita, it got run over," he answered Meche's question. "A bus on Avenida Revolución ran over the guitar and my brother. Yes, it is a pity, but no amount of tears will raise him from the dead."

"Take it, sir," Meche said, her eyes shining. "I have no use for it."

The blindman's loving hands felt the curves of the thing Meche had given him and exclaimed, "A guitar!"

He began to strum on it and raise his spirits, too.

"*¡Ándale!*" he said, moving his body and feet to the sound of an out-of-tune ditty.

"Señorita, can you accompany me a while?" said the blindman. "At this time of the night, the streets are very dangerous for a lone blindman."

"Of course," said Meche, after a moment of reflection. *Válgame Dios*, she thought, *I am going to live, yes, I am going to live, even though I have to make my way robbing coins from a blindman!*

She and the blind guitarist, playing a sad song, walked further into the darkness that congregated on both sides of the border.

Sexy as Hell

Andy Stone got all the scoops. He'd do anything to get a story—lie, cajole, pander, bribe—anything to squeeze a drop of information out of often reluctant sources. Mexico is not terribly open when it comes to the press, and there's no quicker way to get somebody to clam up than saying you work for a newspaper. So, to interview a bank guard, Andy became a banking executive from Los Angeles on a fact-finding mission; to unseal the lips of the police, he often transformed into a murder victim's bereaved next-of-kin.

What drove him, I often wondered, to spend his nights at the office, tapping out front-page stories; his weekends conducting nonstop interviews and pumping sources? Yes, Andy had an abiding honesty, a passion for truth, and a stalwart, resolute nature—but so did we all. With him, it was something more. He never seemed to want to go home. In time the truth was revealed, and I learned his secret. Andy had a bad marriage.

He'd gotten hitched to a former English student of his three years earlier at 7:30 a.m. in a Justice of the Peace's office in Tlaquepaque, an annex of Guadalajara. It was cold that morning. Their breaths made steam and no one joined the ceremony apart from a janitor and secretary raised to the status of witnesses. Afterward, Andy dutifully returned to Guadalajara and taught his 9 a.m. English class. There was no honeymoon in Cancún, he wryly recounted, and his new bride's parents had been dead-set against the marriage.

It was obvious that Beatriz was a holder-inner. There are two kinds of women, the holder-inners and the confiders. Beatriz and nine out of ten Mexican women belong in the first group. She was one to keep things pent-up and not say a harsh word for months, and then all of a sudden, "You know why I'm angry . . ." when it was impossible to know unless you were a mind-reader. Once Andy said, "Today my wife said she married me just to get out of her parents' house." That zinger came out after two years of marriage and one child, two years of Beatriz stewing and being morose. Maybe it was true. It certainly was for a lot of other Mexican women who get pregnant to escape their parents and then chalk it up to God's will. But a sensitive woman never would have said such a thing to a man she loved even a little.

To hear Andy tell it, Beatriz started showing her true colors in the eighth month of pregnancy (sixth, for the benefit of his God-fearing parents). It was when they first flew north of the border to meet Andy's folks, and Beatriz went on a shopping spree at all the swap meets and 99-cent stores, buying teddy bears for her aunts, Barbie dolls for her little half sisters, G.I. Joes for her little brothers, and jumbo bags of laundry detergent and cheese puffs for her mother.

"Beatriz bought five of those metal thingies to curl eyelashes! One or two, yeah, but who needs five?"

"Come on."

"She's got thick lashes, but you gotta be kidding," Andy said. "I blew my top having to hoist a two-ton ghetto blaster for her great grandmother and stow it in the plane's overhead. I never even knew my great grandmother for God's sake. In order to have somebody to buy that many gifts for, I'd have to raise relatives from the dead."

We sent the last page to the printers for that week's edition, and Andy and I decided to go out. It was his last day at the paper, a weekly real-estate rag catering to the area's English-speaking expatriates. To give you an idea, this paper even featured the week's best bridge scores.

We drove in Andy's car to a pool-hall/bowling alley. It was a neon-infused tabernacle to American pop culture frequented by *fresas*, the rich and spoiled, who shot pool in Versace shirts as Jim, Elvis and Janis looked on.

"I'll be sorry to see you go," I said to Andy, taking a pool cue.

"I'm gonna leave tomorrow," he said, "and I'll get there right after Memorial Day. It gives me plenty of time to get a teaching job. Who's going to break?"

"I will," I said, and lined up the balls in the rack. With a loud click the balls scattered helter-skelter over the field of green and one striped ball slid into the corner pocket.

Andy set up a shot after I'd missed mine, and continued as if holding a private conversation with himself:

"Yeah. I'll go first and look for a job. When I get settled, the family's coming up. My wife and I are still having problems." He pushed his glasses up over the bridge of his narrow nose. "Beatriz doesn't want to go with me."

"She's your wife," I said. "She has to go."

"She's very tied to her family and her job," Andy said. Before lining up his next shot, he faced a picture of John Wayne on the wall.

"What would The Duke have done in my case?" he asked. "They say all his wives were Mexican."

"Maybe he'd have spanked her, like he did to Maureen O'Hara in McClintock."

"Didn't see that one. Was it good?"

"Good shot!" I complimented him on an intricate carom he'd engineered.

Andy hunched over, lining up his next one, saying after a sigh, "I don't know how you and Silvia do it.

You seem to get along so well." I nodded in agreement, and Andy asked sternly, "When your wife went to the United States, did she buy any souvenirs?"

"Oh, a few things at Disneyland," I mumbled.

He repeated the story of Beatriz' wild-West shopping spree, and I pretended I was hearing it for the first time. Eyeing a shot down the line of his cue, Andy knocked over one of the *fresa*'s beers at the table behind us. It dribbled down the side of the pool table and pooled on the floor below. A long-haired kid with sideburns gave him a nasty look, and two of his buddies closed in. It looked like we might have to fight these little rich shits.

Sideburns raised his pool cue, and he and his buddies took a step forward. Andy would've rolled up his shirtsleeves if he'd had any to roll up.

"Your press badge, Andy, show 'em your press badge," I whispered.

"Maybe I should call the American Consulate," he whispered back.

Other *fresa* girls and boys looked on expectantly. One of Sideburns' amigos whispered something into his ear and they both looked at Andy.

"My friend says you used to be his English teacher," Sideburns said. "Hot damn."

Andy blinked three times, letting it seep into his brain.

"Where'd you pick that up?" he asked finally. "Did you live in Texas?"

"I got it off the cable TV."

Soon Sideburns and his amigos were buying us beers and trying out their English on us. It turned out one of them had dated Beatriz' sister. He and Andy were practically related—blood brothers.

Andy and I left the pool hall in a frenzy of handshakes and well wishes. It was time to either call it a night or go to another place. We decided on the latter course.

La Fuente was a grungy cantina located in the old part of the city, and it was basically *fresa*-proof, huddled in seedy squalor between the somber stone edifices of Colonial Spain. The roar of hysterically drunk voices and the raucous music of a honky-tonk piano spilled out onto the street from behind the screen that blocked the interior from street view. The only risk to the cantina's integrity came from a new coat of paint applied a few months earlier.

La Fuente drew newspapermen and women from the big daily across the street—so many, the joke went, that the thirsty reporters had tunneled underneath the street to have direct access to it. I hailed a drama critic I knew, but he was so deep into his cups, he probably wouldn't have recognized his own mother.

Andy and I found seats at a table in the rear. We started talking about the odd—mostly geriatric—assortment of characters we'd met at our paper.

"What about Collins?" Andy said. "They must be grooming someone to fill his shoes."

This snowy-haired gent with young brown eyes in an old, wrinkly face had a special beat: the expat community, the American Legion and the American Society. Collins had a unique touch with the old geezers that enabled him to coax information out of them easily. It was rumored that he'd been a spook with the CIA or the OSS. The rumors were probably bullshit, but it was the kind of bullshit that kept things amusing.

"They've got to be grooming someone," Andy said again.

"Nobody lasts forever," I replied.

"Here's to mortality," Andy said. We touched bottles.

"To mortality. The only thing that makes sense of everything."

Our Victoria beers had bright yellow labels. They elicited a comment from Andy:

"In college we believed that if you peeled a label off a beer without tearing it, you could present it to the girl of your dreams, and she would fuck you."

"Have you ever tried it?" I asked.

"No, the girl of my dreams would probably tell me to fuck off."

"So why do you think Collins was with the OSS?"

"You think he's the coolest guy in the world, cool as the Dalai Lama, but he has a temper. And boy, did he get steamed when you asked if he's ever been inside the Pentagon. Imagine those stony eyes, that firm jaw, and ask yourself if he could pull the trigger if it was a matter of national security."

"I wouldn't put it past him. He has a real temper," I sipped my beer. "Joe, on the other hand . . ."

Joe was our proofreader, a man pushing ninety and

more wrinkled than a Chinese bulldog. Hunched over his corner desk, he penciled corrections all day, a cigarette-smoking corpse. The smoke was the only thing that moved.

"I wonder how Joe got the job?" Andy mused.

"He must have lied about his credentials."

"That's the gringo code of ethics in Mexico. Boast, bullshit, brag. If you were a buck private make yourself a general. Make yourself ten times bigger than you ever were back at home. From what I've seen, that's how we operate down here."

"Most gringos you find in Mexico are here because they're not wanted in the States, or they are. That's what Jerry Kinkaid says."

"Jerry should know," said Andy. "What woman in the U.S. would want a loser like that? He felt guilty for inviting Socorro to see his family in the States. For us it's no big deal, inviting a friend or girlfriend to your house. But she got her hopes up and thought that because Jerry had invited her to visit his hometown and meet his parents, he was going to pop the question."

"That's the reason he married her," I said, taking a drink from Andy's bottle. "He felt sorry for her afterward, so he asked Socorro to marry him."

"Jerry belongs to that group that goes back to the United States and can't hack it," Andy said. "You heard about the land he had in New Mexico? He wanted to build a house for his wife and kids. When they got there, it was impossible because of all the permits required and having to hire union plumbers, electricians and bricklayers for every little thing. He couldn't hack it and came back."

"God, Jerry's wife is a witch," I said.

"You got the consonant wrong," said Andy.

"Another beer and we'll call it a night. OK?"

"Yeah, I can't get too wasted. I have to pack in the morning. Hey," Andy exclaimed after counting the change we got back from the waiter, "that guy charged us too much."

"Since you already paid for it, have another."

We signaled the waiter. Andy said, "You know, whenever I hear Jerry talk to his wife it's in broken Spanish. I wonder how they went out on their first date."

"I could talk to Silvia because I'd taken summer classes in Cuernavaca."

"Beatriz and I didn't need words. She was sexy as hell," Andy said with a long face. "That was my wife when I met her. Then it became hell. We're always fighting and I dread going home." He chugged down the rest of his beer. "You know, Beatriz has a full-time executive job that pays 3,000 pesos a month, and she doesn't pay one cent for our bills. Since we got married we keep separate bank accounts. Now, even with me going away, she still wants me to pay the rent. It's ridiculous."

"You'd better put it all in the same pot," I said, "like me and Silvia."

"It must be nice," he said wistfully. "I don't know how you and Silvia do it. It must be nice to get along and make decisions together."

A guy walked up with a shock box, one of those strange Mexican phenomena that you have to have two beers in your gut to appreciate fully.

"Do you want?" he said. "*Recuerdo de Guadalajara.*" The shock vendor extended two shiny chrome bars connected by wires to a shoebox-sized contraption with a dial that controlled the strength of the jolt delivered. The increasing levels were painted on the box in what looked like white-out: *mariposa*, *mandilón* and *macho*, the strongest.

"No gracias," we said. The shock-vendor realized we weren't a couple of good-time foreign students here for summer Spanish classes.

He moved on to the next table, where four light-skinned Mexicans accepted the offer. One of them held the silver chromed tube the size of a hair curler. The rest of them joined hands, with the last man gripping the other metal tube, joined by wires to some kind of battery. The shock vendor turned the dial, which cranked up the volts—first to *mariposa* (fairy), then *mandilón* (hen-pecked husband). His semi-drunk patrons laughed as the current surged through their bodies. Then, just before reaching the macho level, the laughter stopped. They let go of the tubes and waved their smarting hands. When it was over, one decided to try it all by himself. He held the tubes while the vendor turned up the juice higher and higher. His hands gripped the shiny metal bars and the veins bulged in his arms and neck, and he shuddered. Some girls watched out the corners of their eyes, fascinated by the spectacle.

"You have to be drunk to do that," Andy said.

"Yeah," I agreed, "shit-faced drunk."

"I know you're getting drunk," Andy said, "because you don't usually cuss."

Andy gazed off into the bar and commented that in another year this place would be back to its cruddy old self after the paint-job.

"It already looks like they painted it twenty years ago. At least no one tried to change the bicycle."

There it was in its nook above the bar, the legendary bicycle a patron had left as security for an unpaid bar bill fifty years earlier. Nobody ever claimed it, so it became a relic. The bicycle looked prehistoric, soot and nicotine-caked with big flat balloon rubber tires.

"I oughta ride that bike right out of here and out of Beatriz' life. If it were only for my sake I'd leave now, but there's my kid. I never thought I'd love being a father so much. I can change a diaper, feed him, tie his shoes—things I never dreamed I could do," Andy smiled at that thought. "My wife says if I was as good a husband as I am a father, she'd be happy. If it weren't for my boy, I'd leave this second, but he needs a mother and father even if we hate each other."

"A kid senses more than you think," I said. "My parents waited to get divorced until my sister and I were out of high school. Look, a child knows when two adults don't get along. To tell you the truth, my sister and I were relieved when the divorce finally happened."

Over by the bar sat a blond American woman, a queen bee with the Mexican drones.

"I'd peel the label off my beer and give it to her," Andy said and put his hand on his chin. "To level with you, I've thought about cheating on Beatriz. But what's the good? The relationship will never progress beyond a certain point, so there has to be a hidden motive. There would always be lies in the middle of it. 'Honey, I'm working late at the office. I had a meeting with the boss. Honey, I had car trouble on the way home.' Say, Gloria in the office has given me the eye a couple times. Has she ever given you the eye? What do you know about her?"

"She's married to a construction engineer, and you'd probably end up with cement shoes at the bottom of Lake Chapala."

"On the other hand," Andy continued, "some women know their husbands keep mistresses, and they keep living the lie because they're hooked on their lifestyle and getting money to feed the children. They don't want to rock the boat."

Just then a bottle crashed onto the floor and everybody looked around blankly. This was a tacit signal for the place to close. The drunk drama critic's friends hoisted him onto their shoulders, and the crowd moved slowly towards the door.

Outside, I could feel an ocean-sway under my feet as we veered into a dark void. Then there was thumping, a heavy monotonous thumping, that got louder and louder. We weaved around a new corner, and drowned in the thumping and the brightness. Strange hands were feeling Andy and me for weapons, and after a farewell pat from the security guard, darkness again, rich and comforting, with just the faintest taste of manufactured fog. Up on a stage lit by purplish black-light, a busty dancer was doing the shower routine, soaping up her smooth body. The intense, monotonous thump-thumping made talking impossible. There were lots of business types with double-breasted suits looking bored and young guys hot to trot.

"We better get going," Andy shouted over the thumping after just one beer. "My wife would kill me if she knew I was in a place like this."

Around the corner on the Calzada, the broad avenue that divides the city, we were ready to call it a night and go back to Andy's car, once we remembered where he left it. Then Andy's eyes, slightly dulled by beer, spotted Victor's. They brightened. Victor's was a real down and dirty place that Andy hadn't been to since he was single. The paint was peeling and it was possible to see a cockroach climb the wall. Most of the patrons couldn't see that far, though. The place was redeemed by shrimp broth, served between rounds, and a great juke box with old Cuban songs and popular Mexican music— Benny Moré and Pedro Infante. A waiter named Chango brought the beers, and the dead soldiers piled up.

The hookers were gathered by the stools at one end of the bar—old, dumpy and shopworn, dressed in skimpy, shiny clothes. Talking amongst themselves with an air of plotting, they looked over at us from time to time.

"I bet Collins knows who shot Kennedy," I said to keep Andy off the topic of his wife.

"I bet he does too. Why don't we call old Collins to find out."

I reached into my pocket for a coin and handed it to Andy.

"You call," I said, fearing the fury of the former CIA man when we woke him after midnight to ask who shot Kennedy.

"No, you call," Andy said.

A gal with hard eyes and a pock-marked face covered by thick mascara sat down at our table.

"*¿Cómo estás? ¿De dónde son?*" she said, leaning close and putting a hand on Andy's knee.

"Listen, maybe she knows who killed Kennedy."

"Who cares about Kennedy? I want to know who shot officer J.D. Tippit."

"Kennedy, *hombre guapo*," said the hooker.

"Look, we're not interested," Andy said. "We're homosexual lovers."

"It shows," snorted the hooker. She stood up haughtily and went back to join her friends at the bar. After that, she kept giving us odd sidelong glances.

The guy with the shock box entered the bar's swinging doors, looking for customers. He extended the shiny silver tubes to us.

"Oh, what the hell," Andy said, clutching one in his palm. "You take the other one."

We stood and held hands and the electric charge flowed from one body into the next. Eyes glowing, the shock-seller turned the voltage up all the way to *macho*, and I felt the hairs on the top of my head begin to stand on end, and I fought the urge to release my grip. The hooker looked at us with a mixture of curiosity and righteous disgust. The whole affair left an aching, tingling sensation in my joints.

"So I'm leaving tomorrow," said Andy as we walked outside through the swinging doors. The shock box seemed to have sobered us up. We strolled down the dark street that the streetlight only seemed to make darker, and lonelier.

"I'm going it alone, because Beatriz doesn't want to go to the United States with me. Not now." Andy took off his glasses and squinted, while he misted them with his breath and cleaned the lenses on his shirt. "Just the way I came down five years ago with two suitcases, and just as scared," he said, cow-brown eyes wide with disbelief. "As soon as I land a job up there I'm going to call Beatriz and she'll come up with the kid and the furniture. It's not the marriage I care about. I'm worried about my boy—what kind of life he can expect, what kind of friends he'll have. Going to school and having friends in the States is not the same as here. There're so many more dangers: drugs, gangs, peer pressure, things we don't have to worry about in Mexico."

Between the lines I could read that Andy didn't really want to go. We drove several blocks in his car without saying a word.

"Good night," Andy said when we reached my house.

Silvia had left the light on outside.

"Good luck," I replied, clapping him on the shoulder and climbing out of the car.

"Remember," Andy said, "every silver lining has a cloud."

He stepped on the gas and the Arizona-plated car receded down Manuel Acuña until its one red taillight became a blur in the distance. Alone he went, without wife and child. It made a lump in my throat. Goodbye, Andy, old chum, adiós.

It was sad thinking about having to leave a country where life was good but it was impossible to make ends meet. Where people said good morning instead of sneering at each other, and family mattered. The time would come for Silvia and me to make the decision to leave. But that was *mañana*, and now was now, as it always was in Mexico. It's taking a two-week vacation and worrying later about what you'll pawn to pay for it.

I glanced at my watch, and then looked back over my shoulder to see if any of the nosey neighbors were peering out their windows.

I went upstairs to our apartment, where all the lights were on.

"Where were you?" Silvia said. "I was waiting for you, why didn't you call?"

"Stone and I went out. Had a couple beers," I said. "You know Andy is leaving." I noticed Silvia's eyes were red and puffy. "This was his last day at the paper.

He and Beatriz are moving to the United States."

"You've been drinking."

"I told you I was, Silvia."

"I was worried sick. You could have called."

On the kitchen table I saw a cold chicken breast floating in salsa verde. My favorite. Silvia had made it all for me—she didn't even like chicken. Alongside the carefully arranged plate there were colored napkins in teak hoops and a lit candle. Of course I could have called home, and it hurt like hell that I didn't even think of calling. Now I was angry at Silvia and myself, and anything I said at this point would be unsafe.

I put my arms around her and hugged her close. Instead of convincing her that everything was all right, my embrace served to provoke new tears.

"I'm sorry," she said. "I worry about you. I worry about you too much. You could have an accident. Step off the curb and one of these loco bus drivers . . ."

Before she could finish, she choked up again. I pushed a strand of hair away from her eyes.

"It's OK."

"Sometimes I'm afraid to be here all alone and I imagine you with another woman. And it kills me. That woman from the newspaper who sells ads and flirts with all the real-estate men. I saw the way she looked at you at the Christmas party."

"You don't have anything to worry about, Silvia. I'm not a real-estate agent."

Silvia was laughing before the tears had dried.

We sat on the edge of the bed. There were kisses and soft words and buttons undone. Our bodies freed, we melted into each other's arms, rediscovered our bodies. As the aching sweetness soared and overtook us, I saw naked brown flesh, browner than Silvia's, and pillowy breasts starred by iodine teats hanging down in soft lamplight; breasts not Silvia's. They belonged to Beatriz, Andy's wife, sexy as hell, one stupid tequila night while Andy burned the midnight oil at the newspaper.

The memory of Beatriz made me smile and hurt a little too. Silvia thought the smile was for her. It became a part of the solace Silvia and I gained by making love that night after Andy and I went out. I've always wondered if that was the night the twins came to be.

Nostalgia for Death

In our Latin American city there are many old, cavernous houses, still considered "modern" due to certain architectural plagiarisms from Le Corbusier, although they were built thirty or forty years ago. In size and number of bedrooms each outdid the other, housing at the very least a Catholic numerousness of twelve children, and often equipped with side chapels steeped in candlelight and imbued by the perfume of old incense. Today these houses evoke the same *tristesse* that one has contemplating a woman who was a great beauty in her time and now neither cosmetic or surgical artifices work to disguise time's ravages. Weeds strangle their vast gardens; their swimming pools die of thirst; their windows, once messengers of light, are spidered by cracks and covered by plastic tarp; their gently curving stairs that introduced so many ladies to high society, are missing tiles, and a persistent humidity has stained the ceiling with traceries of rust and corrosion.

But all the inroads of deterioration do not affect, not in the slightest, the grand status of the families in those decrepit houses, who continue showing off their surnames untarnished and their glory intact.

Pablo Orendáin grew up in such a house in Colonia Chapalita. Besides being a physician (internal medicine) I also dabble in literature and, to a certain extent, my lively imagination frees me from the shackles and prejudices of my position in society, but in my most perverse fantasies I have not glimpsed the darkness of the human heart that my encounter with the peculiar personage of Orendáin revealed, an encounter that now, after several months have elapsed, I will try to reconstruct. After much reflection, as both a medical and literary man, I have drawn the conclusion that Pablo Orendáin suffered a malady unknown to medical science but quite understandable to those who know the dwellers in the gaping old houses of my city: nostalgia for death . . .

It was the last night of our stay in the charming city of San Francisco, where my wife and I attended a medical conference. To celebrate our last night, we went to the opera. Verdi's enchanting music hugged each and every one present, especially the Hebrew slaves' chorus "Libertad" whose shimmering melody elevates the soul into a sublime sphere, taking one to a golden celestial cloud.

When exiting the theater, we carried the stately, vibrant chords in our breasts and we continued to float, my wife and I, on our little golden cloud. One almost had the foolhardy expectation of being transported to another golden age to the clopping cadence of horsehooves pulling carriages. Our carriage, however, was a dilapidated taxi. Its history of dents and scratches foreboded that we might not be in the steadiest of hands. My wife and I took our places in the back seat, still warm from the body of the last passenger.

"Where to?" the driver asked.

He turned his head to hear the name of our hotel. He closed his eyelids woven with many tiny blue veins, and I saw a long face that possessed a paleness almost phosphorescent in the taxi hugged by the brisk bay night. His black hair was uncombed, or else the wind got to it. He had a narrow bony nose and eyes that protruded from their place in his long head and tended to wander, two black dots on white globes, so it was impossible to tell if he was looking at me or my wife.

"You went to the opera?" the driver said in English with a light accent, as the car lurched forward.

"Where are you from?" my wife asked, the bolder of the two in these situations.

"You'll never guess," he said.

"Greece," my wife posed.

"People think I'm from Greece, Italy, Armenia sometimes, or Syria. You'll never guess. I'm from Mexico."

After this discovery that our driver was from Mexico, we stopped struggling with the language of the Saxons and spoke plain old Spanish.

"What city?" my wife asked.

"Guadalajara."

"Are you from Guadalajara, Guadalajara?" I spoke. "So many of our countrymen abroad claim Guadalajara, but they are from some little rancho in the sticks."

"Guadalajara, I assure you. With the smell of damp earth, like the song says."

Then my wife asked what neighborhood he lived in to establish mutual friends or, better yet blood ties. The people from Guadalajara could be so petty and bothersome at home, but to find a fellow Tapatío abroad was cause for rejoicing.

"I am an Orendáin Luna," said the man at the wheel and, upon hearing it, I made a respectful nod in tribute to our cab driver's pedigree. My wife gasped.

"Sir," she asked, now piqued by curiosity, "how did you become a cab driver?"

That was the question that got Orendáin started:

You see me as a taxi driver, and you marvel how it can be. A member of the distinguished Orendáin Luna family driving a taxi. All of my brothers and sisters have come to occupy positions of prestige and power: they are doctors or lawyers or the heads of this or that government bureau, and here and there a token painter or sculptor who has married into wealth and is therefore excused his artistic eccentricity. Although I grew up in this atmosphere, I was odd man out, I had a more simple aim in life: I wanted to be a waiter, plain and simple. To take people's orders instead of giving them and to provide good service. This was unheard of in the Orendáin Luna clan. Blasphemy. Nobody had ever heard of such a thing, and I wasn't going to let them hear about it, either. It was my little secret.

I finished at the university, with honors. Meanwhile, with the change of political party in power, my siblings' influence grew still greater. The Orendáin Lunas were the talk of the town, and everyone had the same stifling expectations for me, the youngest in the family. With my university degree I would be a very good prospect to warm a chair in the governor's cabinet, or why not the governor's chair? But all this depressed me, and I decided to leave our dreary little rancho and go abroad.

I tried Miami: the humidity asphyxiated me. New York wouldn't hire inexperienced waiters. In Los Angeles it seemed all the waiters' jobs were taken by actors. And finally I came to San Francisco. I saw a sign "Now Hiring," and found the best job in the world. I was a bellboy. It wasn't what I had set my sights on, but it was everything I had ever hoped for. I was a bellboy in a great hotel. There world travelers came and went through our lobby; I did not have to travel the world, the world came to me in the lobby filled with fresh orchids and the sound of a purling fountain. I took their suitcases and accompanied them upstairs. How proud I was of my red uniform, the red of a fresh carnation, and every so often I polished the row of gold buttons in front with the edge of my sleeve, and adjusted my cap on my head and saw myself in the mirror with approbation.

I was an adult, but I was very innocent. On my way home from the hotel, I saw a sign that said adult books. Growing up protected as I had been, I had never seen anything like it. Magazines full of naked bodies doing all kinds of things and other materials to stimulate lustful desires. There were many of these shops in San Francisco, you know, maybe because it's so cold here. I swore I would never enter one of these shops again, but soon enough I was back. Not long after that I overcame my reluctance and entered in more intimate relations, thanks to many opportunities that presented themselves in my job as bellboy. I lost myself in a paradise of flesh. I felt I needed all these arms, breasts, legs, armpits and nipples. You are repulsed by armpits? But what is desired is not always desirable in polite society. I lavished kisses, sighs and caresses as if driven to complete a single love out of a thousand bodies. Above all, a sensation of freedom and anonymity that I had never known in my city intoxicated me. Back home I couldn't drink a beer without someone saying, "Oh did you see Pablo Orendáin Luna in that dive?" Here I was free.

What an ill-fated moment to receive a death sentence, in the bloom of youth, the grip of passions, now tainted by the knowledge of death. I had just discovered the joy of being anonymous, not being watched or judged or expected to behave any certain way, free from the Orendáin Luna dynasty. To be nobody was so refreshing. I was being punished clearly for my sins of the flesh. I believe it was a punishment of God, yes, a punishment of God for all my debauchery, I had to suffer a death that came tiptoeing slowly toward me. You see, the judge gave me the death penalty for killing a policeman. I will not bore you with the tawdry details of the crime. One policeman more or less, it does not matter. Maybe he had a family that loved him, or maybe he was a swine who beat up his wife. And a killer still may have a dog that loves him and wags its tail when he comes home at night. That is beside the point. I was locked up. Days passed like centuries, but there was a reward in my suffering: I reached what can be called "grandeur of spirit," being able to overlook those little irritants that affect life; if the bread was hard, or there was no hot water, it didn't matter. This I had, grandeur of spirit.

If I were not the black sheep of the family I am sure the Orendáin Lunas could have sprung me out of prison in no time. But I was the blackest of sheep in our family and they let me rot. Each day seemed to never end, but when I looked back, the years went in a flash, accompanied by the sound of bars clanking shut and the echoes of feet shuffling through passages. As my execution approached, I was counting the days. I saw it with gratitude, longing for my liberation from this cell three meters across. An end to my suffering. All the tricks of the law to prolong my suffering had been exhausted. Then something incredible happened. Another man confessed to killing the policeman when two detectives came knocking on his door. They had come about a completely different matter—nothing to do with the man. The apple fell off the tree the moment he opened the door and saw the two police detectives standing there. This was the true killer of the policeman I had stumbled upon in front of the hotel, who appeared to be sleeping, and then I picked up the gun that was lying on the sidewalk, still warm. So when I least expected it I was alive and free. I had always expected to be free but not alive. It came time to leave the prison and breathe the air outside.

I crossed the road and boarded a bus for San Francisco, my shoulders lost in a polka dot shirt two sizes too big for me. In a bundle I held my bellboy uniform, now faded, its buttons rusty.

I lived such intense moments, observing the passengers. I was still in a daze. My eyes hurt, unused to seeing all I was seeing. The bright sunlight slashed through the side windows of the bus. A boy with headphones moved his head to the beat of an unheard tune, next to an old lady with heavy shopping bags for suitcases; a harried mother carried a baby on her legs; there were two nuns with their nun hats (they didn't smile) and a fat man with a beret and a placid expression. I gazed raptly at all their faces, and I realized that they were joined by one thing: a sad sediment in the bottom of their eyes. They were in the jail of sadness while the joy of having escaped death flooded my heart. I had to share the joy with someone.

That chance came when I got off the bus in San Francisco. There a red-cheeked old woman in a woolly overcoat gave me an enormous hug, and she offered me a sip from her pocket bottle. People on the street looked at me as if I was crazy. This day I cried. I cried from pure happiness seated on the edge of the sidewalk. Time froze; youth and beauty showed luminous through all things with a divinity, yes, a pulsating divinity. There were children blowing bubbles, and they floated across the sky till they burst or a twig punctured them, sweethearts kissing for the first time, and the sun blowing through the trees swaying in sympathy as the daffodils danced, the mist from a park fountain blew against my face, tickling my nose, and my gratitude for being alive was renewed. It was heartbreakingly beautiful and tender, a moment filled with such love and tenderness as I have ever known, seated there on the edge of the sidewalk. Alive.

Eventually I got a job at a hotel without stars. At first I proudly wore my old uniform. But others at the hotel made fun of its formality. I began to seek the comfort of alcohol, and I began to long for the days when I believed I was going to die in prison. I was going to die, so each breath was precious, each act entailed so much nobility of life against death, the nobility to bear each petty annoyance without a single complaint. I craved to return to that time when to smile was to be brave. Now I am irked by hard bread, hot and cold, warm beer and long lines. I miss that heroic time in prison terribly. The moment overflowing with gratitude was so fleeting. I miss the certainty of death and the cold reliability of its embrace. That is the joke of it all, the last laugh, that is death's prerogative: having once escaped by the skin of my teeth, sooner or later, the old whore reaper will come back to bite me again. But I am going to outfox it. Yes, I am.

You asked me, sir, how I got to be a cab driver. Well. It's very easy, really. In this kind of work I deal with thieves, addicts and crazy people, sometimes nice people, and crazy people who would ordinarily nice but are driven jagged by circumstance. Maybe one of them is a smiler with a knife, and will put an end to my suffering. I am too weak to do it myself. But if someone does it for me, they will be doing me a favor, honestly . . . I am sorry. So sorry for having talked so much. I am a wretched man, less human than a dog. It was a terrible indiscretion. Do you forgive me? I beg you. Thank you, kind souls, for listening . . . I trust that my melancholy has not tarnished your stay in this beautiful city. Here we are, we've reached the entrance to your hotel. Fifteen dollars, please.

The Hit

The Granma, the yacht crammed with Castro's rebels, readied for launch from the coast of Veracruz. They were to set sail shortly after midnight on November 25, 1956, when a deafeningly loud smell—as human and fetid as shit—filtered down through the starry sky. The rag-tag band of 80-plus guerilla fighters aboard the Granma, a yacht built to accommodate only twelve, fled up onto deck, holding their noses, and all vomited profusely . . .

Cassidy angrily yanked the sheet of paper from the typewriter and crumpled it up. Then he proceeded to change the baby's diapers and eliminated the cause of the cosmic stench.

"Let's go for a walk, baby," Cassidy said.

Cassidy left his Olivetti portable and loaded the baby onto a stroller and pushed him out to the sun-drenched street, toward the plaza. He brought along no books or notepads, as he had no delusions of doing any work on his book, a memoir of his adventures in Cuba during the Revolution. Cassidy had known Castro and Che Guevara personally. He wrote for the wire services and helped establish the legend of Castro, the boyish, charismatic, bearded young lawyer and revolutionary, who captivated the American reading public. You have to peel away the layers of history to see how it was, that it began not at all like it turned out. With Castro it began with goodwill for the underdog, honest admiration and plain old entertainment value, a lot of entertainment, which can never be overlooked as an ingredient for a successful revolution. Cassidy knew that people who read the news liked to escape from drab lives into the headlines, and Castro was Cuba's Robin Hood, straight out of Cassidy's boyhood reading. Castro was also David to Batista's Goliath.

In his own first-hand account of the revolution, Cassidy promised to set the record straight.

The plaza café was uncrowded at 11 in the morning. From his vantage, at the wooden table on the yellow wood chairs with woven hemp seats, he could spy on the curio shop where Deborah worked for a bouffant American lady. She was occupied in showing pieces of Taxco silver jewelry to a beak-nosed man in a straw hat. A woman in a flamingo-pink pantsuit was trying to entice the man into purchase of the silver necklace and he strode off. She tugged on his arm and he came back in reluctant surrender and dug down for his wallet.

Cassidy sat dawdling over the newspaper, a two-week old *New York Times* yellowed by the time the pack-mules got it to the village. Allende had just won big in Chile—a victory for the people. The Americans were still reeling from Tet. Cassidy didn't much like the Vietnam war, but sometimes he itched to be in the thick of action again.

He lit up a Delicado and drew the smoke into his lungs.

"Hi there," a man's voice interrupted his tobacco- and caffeine-induced reverie. Cassidy looked over and saw a man with long stringy hair and a wild, uncombed beard that nearly obscured the chrome peace sign that hung over the purple and yellow neon of his tie-dyed shirt. "I know you," the hippie said knowingly.

Cassidy peered over the edge of his paper. "Maybe you know my doppelgänger."

"Were you ever in New Haven?" the stranger asked.

Mention of the city, home to Yale University, gave Cassidy a start.

"Your name is John," said the stranger.

Cassidy was freaking out.

"And you come from Braintree and you never learned to whistle."

". . . Buzz," Cassidy exclaimed after what felt like forever.

He got up across the table and hugged the bearded stranger.

"Look at you," Cassidy repeated. "Back in New Haven, *I* was the boho."

Fueled by the recognition of his first-year roommate, Cassidy laughed and chattered away. The bearded man told him how he had traveled to India and lived in an *ashram*. Cassidy told him how he had gotten married and had a baby.

Cassidy invited his friend, Buzz Lowell, to stay at their cottage. Even though it was cramped, Cassidy wouldn't take no for an answer and have his friend stay at the overpriced inn down the road. During the nights and days that followed, they laughed and chattered, smoking grass and increased their knowledge of tequila and mezcal. Deborah would partake sometimes, but mostly she retired early to nurse the baby, and she had to get up in the morning to go to the curio shop.

Tossing in bed, she could hear the stoned hum of Buzz and Cassidy's midnight colloquies through the curtain that served as bedroom door.

"It's like Che said, create 100 Vietnams, 1000 Vietnams to bring about change," Buzz would say. "You should go to Chile, that's where it's happening."

"Marx cannot save the world. He's talking about material salvation, and we're talking about souls. You should understand that, Buzz. You lived in an *ashram*."

On and on they went through the night. They would be asleep on the couch, noses up to the world and mouths open, when a glowering Deborah put on her cheery sundress and set off in the morning.

Any house guest is a disruption. Cassidy abandoned work on his book, and Deborah began to get rattled by Buzz' rampant guru-like presence. Little things undermined a fragile sanity: the keys weren't on the hook on the wall, her shampoo bottle was down to the last green drops. Peanut butter—impossible to get in Mexico—was scraped to the bottom of the jar. A brand-new jar Deborah's mom had just shipped from the States. At night, after getting home from work, she would yearn to take a long hot bath and all the hot water would be used up.

Finally, the tension came to a head one morning at the curio store, which had become the sole place where Cassidy and his wife still had any measure of intimacy. Cassidy stopped by and Deborah was waiting on some manta-wearing hippies. Seeing him, she exploded, "Buzz has got to go. Eating our food and using my shampoo. And political discussions at all hours. See the bags under my eyes?"

Cassidy couldn't, but he wasn't going to argue with her. The customers were taken aback by Deborah's outburst and retreated down the street.

"You're drinking so much, John. And smoking pot. Are you even working on your book? I'm the only person who is working in this household."

Cassidy had an urge to smash the blown-glass goblets that filled the shelves into smithereens. The urge passed; he mastered it. This self-control fed the illusion that Cassidy was a better man than his hothead Irish father had been. He also recognized that Deborah had a point.

"I'll talk to Buzz," he said weakly.

◆ ◆ ◆

Anguished, Cassidy invited Buzz out to walk the cobbled streets. They ate *charral*, the local specialty of fried minnows, at a stand near the pier, as he steeled himself to drop the bomb. As soon as they finished eating, he would bring up the matter of Buzz overstaying his welcome.

Cassidy cleared his throat. "Buzz, it's been great having you here..." Before Cassidy completed his thought, Buzz interrupted.

"I was thinking of leaving and renewing my travels," Buzz said out of the blue. "There's a commune in Guanajuato I want to visit."

Now flooded by sudden relief, Cassidy was saying the exact opposite of what he had dreaded saying.

"Please stay."

"I'm sorry, but it's time to move on." Buzz said. "You know the zen saying: Be as the water."

"I'll miss our late-night discussions."

That night, despite Cassidy's hollow imprecations, Buzz packed up his rucksack and left on the clanking bus. Now Cassidy had peace and quiet in abundance. The Granma was able to launch from Yucatán and bring the seeds of revolution to Cuban shores. And his worts-all history was going to make it ten-weeks on the *Times'* bestseller list; Cassidy felt sure he had a hit on his hands.

A few weeks after Buzz' departure, a postcard came, postmarked Santiago, Chile. In it Buzz painted a glowing picture of the spirit of the people after Allende's election, ready to forge a new socialistic future together. It ended, "When are you going to join us, John?"

Not any time soon. The whole thronged world of the Cuban revolution assailed Cassidy. It was there whenever he wanted it, and sometimes when he didn't. The manuscript pages mounted. He could feel the warm velvet breeze blowing off the Caribbean, the bullets whizzing through the jungle, inches from his head, feel their whooshing wake against his cheek.

The baby was crying. Cassidy was scrambling down mountain paths beside the troops in raggedy, mended clothes. They secured town after town as they approached that day of rejoicing when streamers would shower down from the Havana sky and the crowds would greet them as liberators and heroes . . .

Deborah got home from the curio shop and kissed Cassidy on the cheek.

"Hi, honey," she said. The baby stopped crying when it got into Deborah's arms.

"How can you leave the baby crying!" she scolded Cassidy. "Couldn't you tell he was hungry? And his diapers!"

He left his work table and went to the kitchen. He put cubes of ice into a glass and poured himself a drink, took two shallow gulps and then polished it off in one swig. He put new ice into the empty glass.

"You keep drinking like that," Deborah said, "pretty soon you won't be able to write your own name."

She pulled up her shirt gingerly and the baby suckled.

"I'm going out for a smoke," he left in surly silence.

Cassidy walked up the cobbled street, away from the lake. He crossed the plaza. A breeze was blowing cool off the lake, and there was a new moon. The breeze stirred blue-and-white tissue papers with lacey cut-outs, leftover fiesta festoons that draped down from the church steeple.

He felt drawn into the church. One side of the carved wooden doors was open. He slipped inside the cool tiled and incense-laden sanctum, cream and gold splashed and full of painted saints. Cassidy kneeled. He said a prayer for Deborah and for his son. He said a prayer for all the poor bastards who were bleeding in Vietnam. He said a prayer for himself. Enlighten us, oh Lord.

He suddenly felt he was not alone in the church, but looking around he saw no one. Outside, he lit up a Delicado. The acrid smoke drifted over his shoulder and his feet moved over the cobbles, wet and shiny from the afternoon rain.

As he continued his walk, down toward the pier, he sensed again a live presence and stopped cold. He heard the click of a leather sole on wet cobbles. He took a few more steps and waited for the split-second delay. He turned and saw only the darkened windows of the sleeping street. Maybe the adobe walls were echoing his own footfalls. He finally reached the pier. The gondola-like fishing boats bobbed softly on the dark surface of the lake. Cassidy wheeled around.

Nothing. Off in the distance he saw the lantern light of the last plaza vendor reflected off the cobblestones. Then that light went out.

Cassidy had been walking now for maybe half an hour. He put off going home and hoped that Deborah was already asleep. After the rain there were stars, more stars above the village than he had seen crammed into one night. He gazed up at them for a while and felt release from all the pressures of Deborah, the baby and his book.

As his gaze returned to earth, he saw a large head on narrow shoulders limned by the starlight, and kept on going. "John," a voice said. Cassidy knew that voice, but he turned and saw a stranger.

" . . . Buzz?"

Buzz had cut his hair and shaved his beard. He no longer looked like a hippie, but it was Buzz. He had also shed his tie-dyed shirt and wore clothes very similar to Cassidy's own: khakis and a button-down short-sleeve shirt.

"What happened to your hair?" Cassidy exclaimed. "Aren't you supposed to be in Chile?"

"I was in Chile, and I came back." He caught his breath, which seemed more labored from nerves than exhaustion.

"Are you OK? You don't look a bit well, Buzz," Cassidy said. "Maybe you should sit down."

They sat together on the edge of the pier, their feet

kicking into the air. For a moment they were Huck Finn and Tom Sawyer.

Buzz began to mumble.

"Rich crazy Cubans. I met them at a cocktail party in Palm Beach. For some reason they thought I was CIA. I bragged about how well I knew you, the famous journalist and forger of the Castro myth. The Cubans were impressed. Very impressed."

"Oh yeah?"

"Pretty soon they hired me to take care of you."

"Take care of me?"

"Do I have to spell it out, John?"

"You *are* being rather cryptic."

". . . Off, liquidate, deep six, whack, pop, bump off . . ."

"Oh," Cassidy said. He tried to keep a serious face. It was impossible to think of Buzz as a killer, much less a hired killer.

"They think you're a dangerous man."

"They must be sore about the Castro articles," Cassidy said and shook his head. "I'm sore about the Castro articles. Why do you think I'm writing my book? That, and to make some dough."

"Cassidy, always the poor enterprising boy from Braintree, behind the Bohemian pose."

"Why the hell did you get mixed up in a thing like this, Buzz?"

"The money."

"I thought Daddy was loaded."

"I thought so too. Then he blew his brains out and

there were nothing but debts . . . The Cubans offered fifteen thousand in cash. When they see your obituary they'll deliver the money to a safe deposit box in Miami. But I can't do it, I can't. I can't go through with it."

With a gesture of surrender he took a small pistol from his pants pocket and slammed it onto the plank of the pier between them.

Buzz put his head in his hands and sobbed, "I can't do it, I can't." Cassidy reached over and gently took the pistol in his hand. It had a heavy silencer on one end.

"Don't feel bad, Buzz. You're not a killer," he said softly. "Some people don't have it in them. When I was a boy I couldn't wait to get my hands on a .22. I wanted it so bad I could taste it. I begged my dad and begged him. Finally he let me use it. And I shot a blackbird, knocked it right out of the sky. We found it on the ground, its black feathers shiny with blood. That ugly old bird fighting for its last breath and I had to pull the trigger one more time. After that, I never wanted to shoot another living thing."

Buzz smiled sadly, listening to Cassidy.

"That's how I feel," Buzz said. "I can't do it. Even if it's true what they said about you."

Cassidy looked over.

"The Cubans said you were supplying reports to Batista's regime about the locations of rebel munition stashes."

Any self-control Cassidy had exerted to spare the glass goblets now fled as he took the pistol and squeezed. The silencer made a pleasant ping as a firing pin sent a .9 mm bullet on its appointed journey. Buzz' jaw fell slack. He slumped over and lay spread out on the planks of the pier, staring emptily at the starlit sky.

"Batista paid me good money," Cassidy said over Buzz' body. "But I wasn't going to give them any real information. Like everybody else, I was rooting for the rebels."

Cassidy had to be fast now—fishermen would be out in a couple more hours. He splashed a bucket of water over the bloodied part of the pier and rowed out into the middle of the lake with the fresh body aboard. Just before pushing Buzz' body over the edge of the boat, Cassidy riffled his pockets and got his wallet. He pocketed his passport, an airplane ticket to Miami and seized a little round key. A safe-deposit key. He switched his wallet into Buzz' pocket and put his gold wedding band on the dead man's finger.

By the time a fisherman found Buzz' body a couple weeks later, nothing would be left of his face and fingerprints. Deborah would see that gold ring and immediately sink into grieving. Cassidy would be basking on the warm sands of the South Pacific, a new woman at his side and fifteen thousand dollars richer.

Rivals

The whole Colonia del Fresno knew that María Guadalupe had two boyfriends. She had broken up first with Martín, and it had been true as true when she told Pedro that she and Martín weren't seeing each other any more, but Martín wanted to see María Guadalupe just one more time to explain something. He saw her once and found an excuse to see her again, drawing out the matter, and so there began, all quite innocently, the arrangement: she parted from Pedro at eight-thirty, Martín got off from the bicycle repair shop at nine and the two boyfriends never crossed paths.

During the years she was with Pedro and, later with Martín, they held hands passionately every night in the tender shadows of the garden gate, while the trains came and went in the distance, and neither of the two boyfriends had been able to spend a single moment alone with María Guadalupe. Despite repeated attempts to reach the solitude of the roof or the space where the family car was parked, there was always a little sister, a cousin, *some*body around.

María Guadalupe was going to turn fifteen, and everyone wondered which of the two boyfriends would be the *chambelán*, her escort, for the *quinceañera*. To complicate matters, María Guadalupe told both they had been chosen for the coveted role of *chambelán*. Both Martín and Pedro believed they were going to accompany the lovely fifteen year old on her special day. Before disillusioning one boyfriend or the other, however, María Guadalupe died. An insidious bacteria attacked her brain, after she consumed a spoiled strawberry, and that was that. Her agony was devastatingly brief: one moment the young lady vibrated with life and the next, her soul eloped on a long journey aboard one of the trains that go by the Colonia del Fresno. Drowned by flowers and dressed in her *quineañera* gown, she looked more radiant and lovelier than ever in her coffin: a contented expression on her face after having successfully dodged the matter of who would be *chambelán* at her sweet fifteen birthday party.

During the burial in the Panteón Guadalajara, for which the whole colonia turned out, Martín sobbed in silence. In contrast, Pedro came to the edge of the open hole in the ground and shrieked, "*¡Mi niña! ¡Mi niña!*" Three beefy men had to drag him kicking from the grave and, even so, he leaped two more times, and the third time he accomplished his aim of "going with his baby," and suffered a concussion.

How strange, Martín thought. Pedro is very sad. He seems sadder than me. And three years had gone by since Pedro and María stopped seeing each other. How strange.

That night after the burial, Martín could not sleep. The idea of going to the cemetery to see María Guadalupe had gotten into his head and it wouldn't go away like the fly that keeps colliding against a window. Although the cemetery was locked up, the compulsion to go there kept him awake. He waited for the last light to go off in his parents' house and tiptoed out. He took along a rope, a slingshot and two hooks. Everything that he needed to climb the cemetery walls that soar so high to keep out afflicted people like Martín as much as to keep in the unhappy spirits that roam there.

Martín pedaled to the cemetery and left his bicycle at the foot of the enormous wall. He gravitated to the deepest shadow and hurled the rope high above, like a mountain climber. Due to the difficulty of pulling his weight up the rope, Martín gave up, but before heading home, he cast a final glance at the wrought-iron cemetery gate. There hung a padlock. A closer look revealed that the padlock was unjoined and the pieces moved easily apart. It was a miracle! Martin's sneakers hurried through the paths that run between the sumptuous tombs of the powerful and the humble mounds of babies. At last, he came to María Guadalupe's fresh plot. He stopped and breathed in the thick smell of freshly shoveled earth. Everything was quiet as a cemetery.

"Listen," a voice from behind.

Martín's heart stopped. Frightened to death, he didn't want to know if the voice belonged to the living or the dead. Finally, after dominating his fear, he turned and saw Pedro, his rival for Lupe's affections, with a bandage on his head.

"What are you doing here, man?"

"I wanted to be here with María Guadalupe."

"I wanted to be with her," said Pedro. "I saw her lying in the box today, as if she was only asleep and her eyes were about to flutter open. She was so beautiful, I wanted to lie down by her side forever."

They were Martín's exact sentiments, and he was quick to ask:

"Were you in love with Lupe?"

"Hopelessly. She was almost ready to turn fifteen years old, and I was going to be her *chambelán*."

"Are you crazy?" Martín snapped. "Lupe promised me I was going to be *chambelán* more than a month ago. Don't lie."

"It isn't a lie," Pedro said with tears of rage in his eyes.

Oh my, Martín thought, how liars can resort to every kind of shameless trick to awaken sympathy.

"You have repaired your last bicycle, Martín," Pedro said and he closed his hands around Martín's neck.

"I am going to split your head, man. You will lie at María Guadalupe's side forever . . . I am suffering the greatest disillusion of my life, man, realizing that my girlfriend was a lying phony. This is worse than death. I will never fall in love again. Never ever ever," Martín hissed, while he and Pedro mutually squeezed the blood from their necks. "I will never fall in love again because of you."

Pedro felt something long and hard against his stomach.

"What is this?" he asked. "I feel something against my stomach."

The question caught Martín off guard.

"It's a bottle of tequila."

"Are you sure it's not a salami?"

"What are you saying, man?"

"Nothing, *puñal*," Pedro said, using a slur against Martin's masculinity.

"Say that again to my face."

The two of them stepped apart, taking their hands off their necks, like two boxers that go to each corner of their ring. Panting, Martín took out the bottle that he had safeguarded in his pants, took off the cap, and drank. Propping himself on his hands, Pedro kneeled over the fresh tomb, head hung down. He babbled:

"María Guadalupe was the purest, the most beautiful creature in the world, and now I realize that she deceived me when she said you two had broken up. And she went on deceiving me for three years," he sobbed and the dirt sucked his tears. "My baby! Oh, my poor baby!"

The tequila had been for Martín and for him alone, to deal privately with the loss of María Guadalupe, but seeing Pedro in such a bad way got to Martín. He offered him the bottle of tequila. The boy needed the consolation that it brought. Then they passed the bottle between the two without saying a word. At the end of a long while without saying anything, Pedro said:

"Do you remember that nasty hag Aunt Altagracia who always watched over us?"

"Who could forget?" Martín said.

"She was one-eyed, with warts on her nose but she watched over us like a buzzard with that one bloodshot eye."

Yikes, Martín thought, the guy really had been seeing Maria Guadalupe. He knew her great aunt Altagracia. I'm going to kill him, the cretin. And he pictured him dead already, with his mouth open, and bleeding over the fresh grave . . . But before Martín could stick the hook in his back, Pedro began to unburden himself about María Guadalupe's other protectors, besides Aunt Altagracia, who policed their nightly visits. Both Pedro and Martín soon discovered they had plenty in common. With shared hatred, ever more passionate, their two grieving souls united when remembering Uncle Leobardo's bad breath, the slippery gaze of closeted Cousin Pánfilo, old Anacleta's sermons urging the priesthood on Pedro and Martín, the evil eye of the witch Pomponia: one look promised hell to pay if one of them should ever touch María Guadalupe improperly.

"Now they can't do anything," Martín proclaimed, raising his half empty bottle high.

"Nothing," Pedro reiterated with vehemence. "We could fornicate from dusk to dawn with María Guadalupe if we felt like it. "

"But . . ."

". . . she has died."

The two sobbed on each others' shoulders for ten minutes. Then they finished the tequila and began to see a commotion in the east where the sun was rising.

"You know something?" Martín said.

Both looked at each other.

"What?"

Martin took one of the steel hooks as if he was going to stick it in Pedro's back, but he gave him a gentle pat on the cheek.

"You are a good friend."

"You are a good friend, too, man."

Angels

A cotton-candy dusk gathered in the caverns between buildings as office workers fled their daily prisons, Wadyka amid the weary herd. I wondered if I'd recognize him. After all, it had been four years—that's a lot of blood under the bridge. That summer he was interning in an East Side law firm.

"Hey, Woods," Wadyka called out, recognizing me first, despite my longish hair. We met up on the teeming sidewalk, jostled on all sides by emancipated workers.

After exchanging pleasantries, Wadyka offered to carry my suitcase. I shouldered my backpack, and we strolled on into the East Sixties and Seventies. Leaves fluttered on the trees in the side streets; they made a sizzling sound like eggs on a fry pan. There was the promise of coolness in the air. Wadyka and I jabbered non-stop and joked as if we bumped into each other yesterday. A lot had happened in four years. I dropped out of school and left New York to see the world (i.e. work in a shoe store by day, get stoned at night). Wadyka had gotten a law degree. His hairline showed the first signs of thinning and there was the hint of crows feet. Great moons of sweat formed in the underarms of my pinpoint Oxford cloth shirt. I wondered if Wadyka could see defeat behind my smile.

During my tenure at a fraternity on 113th Street, I became acquainted, vaguely, with a fellow who'd been coxen on the Trinity rowing team. His name was something like Tribble or Trippler? My memory is a bit hazy after all that's gone down. The short of it: the extenuated web of friendship obliged a near stranger to put me up for a few days in the sweltering heat of a New York summer.

Wadyka and I reached our destination, the corner of East Seventy-eighth Street and Lexington. Up one flight of stairs to the air-conditioned lair of the former coxen of the Trinity rowing team.

The years had made the coxen more polished and stiffer: he sported a sharkskin suit and had the cold, hard gaze of a junk bond salesman on the make. Just what he was. In the cool rooms the sweat dripping on my back turned pleasantly icy.

As soon as we got to his flat and I phoned a fellow Memphis boy who went to Columbia, Mike Powers, but his line was busy. Mike was also known as the

Hyperbolic Man because you could never quite swallow whole what he said. Among the truth-stretching feats were: shaking hands with John Lennon's killer in Central Park, losing his virginity on the roof of the Ritz Hotel when an elderly aunt hauled him and his brother around Europe and North Africa, and orgiastic parties attended around Elvis' swimming pool as a teen. Maybe there is less truth than poetry in what Mike said, but it was funner to believe than to doubt—and that is the mark of a gifted liar.

Through the Memphis grapevine I knew Mike has just returned from the city of Abu Dhabi—something to do with his job. I use the word *knew* loosely, for it implies a degree of certitude, and Abu Dhabi could have been invented by hyperbolic Mike.

Wadyka and I left my bags in the coxen's apartment and we stole off to a favorite haunt, Pedro's. The moment of naked truth was upon us; it couldn't be postponed. The bartender waited for my order with impatience, tapping his fingers on the counter:

"Well, what'll it be?"

"Iced tea," I spoke up at last.

"We don't have no iced tea. Call Jackson Hole."

"Make it water with a lemon peel."

"Not having a drink? Is your name Jed Woods?" Wadyka said. "Get this man a shot of Wild Turkey!" he shouted to the bartender in that voice reminiscent of Thurston Howell.

"Water," I said. "Make it water."

Wadyka's dubious brow arched, his eyes glared, and he said, "What happened to you, sport?"

"Rehab," I said, studying the table's fake woodgrain, then studying Wadyka's face for any change. "Been clean for three months, knock on formica."

After a several glasses of icewater with a lemon peel, I called Mike Powers again. Pedro's was a speck of a place with an ornate pressed-tin ceiling a few inches above the patrons' heads. The entire menu consisted of the phone number to Jackson Hole, a burger joint across the street, scrawled on a slate over the bar. It was hard to speak on the payphone over the jukebox blare, the patrons' yakking and the toilet flushing, much less trying to talk over the payphone located just outside the john.

Over the bar noise I managed to make out two words muttered in a drunken slur. One was "Fuck" and the other "You" before the payphone sucked up my quarter. That was the Hyperbolic Man; I'd get back to him soon as Wadyka and I finished visiting.

Mike's line was busy that night. Then my host at Seventy-eighth and Lexington, the former coxen from Trinity and future Ivan Bosky, informed me he had a date on Thursday. Her name was Caitlin. Would I mind crashing somewhere else that night? We agreed that if I saw a red thumbtack outside his door Thursday night when returning from my forays, I was to stay someplace else.

On the basis of this man-to-man understanding I developed a warmer, friendlier feeling for my host, and we sealed the red-tack agreement by doing lines of Peruvian coke on the coffee table. The coke was a transgression, but it was terrific and, besides, it would have been rude for a Southern Gentleman like myself to spurn the coxen's hospitality.

The next morning when the euphoria wore off, the elusive Hyperbolic Man loomed larger. Shit, I'd waited too long. I'd called just to say hello, and now I'd be hitting him up for a place to stay. I got a message that his phone was disconnected, so I called his family in Memphis.

"Hi, this is Jed, a friend of Mike's from Columbia," I said. "I've been trying to reach Mike for two days. Who's this?"

"This is Mike's aunt."

There was something funny about that woman's voice. She hardly sounded like the sassy aunt who hauled Mike and his brother around half of Europe and North Africa.

"I've been calling Mike off and on for the last two days, and keep getting a busy signal. Do you—"

The aunt cried out, a plaintive warble, "Mike is dead."

That small tearful voice far away in the swampy city of Memphis, behind the impenetrable kudzu wall, had a delayed effect. That's hyperbolic for you! Mike with the wild blue eyes behind lame plastic aviator frames, the booming crazy mad-scientist's laugh and shock of untamable hair. Mike convincing everybody he was dead. Then that warbling voice came back from behind the kudzu wall, strange and throbbing to remind me of the uneasy situation at hand:

"Mike is dead."

"Can I talk to his dad or mother?"

The aunt told me it would be better to call later, so I left my condolences and number in New York.

I looked out the curtained window at the brick flanks of other buildings and the market below and through the streaks of tears saw the greengrocer spraying heads of lettuce and radishes all neatly piled. Dead. What if Mike took his own life? No way. AIDS? The rumor mill would've gotten to that one. Overdose? Unlikely. Maybe he'd been robbed at pistol point, and Mike regretted not bringing enough money to make a mugger happy. No, the man always boasted of carrying a $ 500 wad . . .

I knew one thing. I needed a drink. A serious drink. I was proud of myself, though, as my hand reached for Trippler's bottle of Chivas, I reached over with the left and pulled the right hand slowly down.

There was plan B, calling another hometown friend who lived in Brooklyn. We were both in the same Memphis University School class and I figured he could be relied on in a pinch, so I dropped by the bookstore where Marcus was working. We spoke animatedly. When I brought up staying at his place, his Brooklyn abode shrank to a broom closet. It wouldn't work,

Marcus said, and went back to dusting the tops of hard-cover books.

Well, I was shit out of luck. My finances were such that I had enough for a hotel room for one night in New York or a five-day Ameripass bus ticket, but not enough for both.

Thursday rolled around.

The coxen's big night, and I still hadn't lined up another place to crash, and I didn't know for sure whether I needed one: everything depended on the red thumbtack. I sought refuge in the bar at the Plaza Hotel. I have always been drawn to this place: outside the picture window horse-drawn cabs and top-hatted drivers with frock coats glided past, the carriage wheel spokes made invisible, and leafy deep-green shadows gathered over Central Park across the way.

The waiter smirked when I asked for an iced-tea, so I ordered a martini instead. Just one. Each sip of chilled martini I let linger on my tongue, thrill my palate, saving the plump green olive for last. It had been so long, that martini had quite a kick. I drunk dialed an old girlfriend, Valerie, living on Park Avenue. Moving up in the world. That first martini opened the door to another, and then one more ... No, I stopped. I stopped at one while my imagination ran off. Had to be strong.

Feeling guilt for this alcoholic respite, I returned apprehensively to the flat on Seventy-eighth and Lexington. Even before gaining the top of the stairs I saw it: a red thumbtack. Vomited to the streets, I started walking, walking, heading down sterile Park Avenue. Treeless stone and masonry: it's a joke they call it Park Avenue.

I crossed over to the West Side via Central Park South and edged up Central Park West, scrupulously avoiding Broadway because it goes at an angle and would shorten my journey. My sole intent was to draw things out just as I lingered over every sip of cold martini in the Oak Room.

Treading up Central Park West, the turreted foreboding, turreted Dakota apartments came into view. One December in 1980 we were watching TV in the dorm, and Mike Powers jumped up and bellowed pointing to the TV, "It's him! It's him!" Earlier that afternoon Mike had strolled past the Dakota and an odd-looking fellow standing in front asked him for the time. It was John Lennon's attacker.

I headed west to Amsterdam Avenue, a preserve of the old kitchen-sink New York. The Avenue had certainly changed, though. Puerto Rican families sweaty loitering around front steps of tenements, ragamuffins playing stickball, and the longing desolation of shirtsleeve men with elbows on the upper-story window sills as the women gossip and watch children from the stoop, all deleted and exchanged for sidewalk tables under scalloped awnings and the well-groomed young, trading glances over drinks.

It was ten o'clock by my watch and a long night lay ahead. After 100th Street I really slowed the pace, taking child-steps. A breeze stirred, fleshy and cool against my greasy skin now that the heat of day had subsided.

The combination of martini at the Plaza and being left on the streets had melted my anti-drinking resolve. I headed for a dive on Broadway, the Marlin Café. It was called a café, although I don't recall ever seeing any cooking there. Stepping into that smoke-choked den on Broadway I came upon a surprising number of known faces. Gideon, Matt and Michael were where I'd left them four years ago; they hadn't changed or moved an inch, sans winter overcoat, of course. They still managed to infuse their bright summer clothes with a hip depressive quality. After a brief effusion of greetings, I bought a round and we caught up on who was doing what in what graduate school and who had slashed their veins or taken too many pills.

When I told them Mike Powers had died, they seemed rather blasé. Of course, the people at the Marlin weren't Mike's crowd at all, and they shed no light on the enigma of his death.

My old friends bought more beers, I reciprocated with another round and noted with concern that my wallet is getting down to that last bill—a counterfeit I'd got back in change once and had never been able to pass on. The numbers and Andrew Jackson's haughty stare were excellently engraved, but something about the too-vivid green aroused suspicion, and I had always kept the bogus bill as a perverse kind of rabbit's foot. Now I was tempted to pass it off on the bartender Jimmy, it would be easy in the bar's shadowy recesses. I was pondering this option when Jimmy shouted, "Last call!" and the Marlin's lights blinked on and off, banishing the enchantment of darkness. We fled like bugs exposed to the sun when a rock is kicked away.

So long, *auf wiedersehen*, till we fuck with each other again. And I felt ashamed, playing the role of traveler, but after seeing these people for the first time in four years, I just couldn't bring myself to ask for a place to crash. Fucking pride.

Outside, somebody had taken trouble to hail a cab for me. I waved it on down Broadway, having no use for a cab. The driver gave me the finger. I started on foot down the great Avenue, with its many moods and caesura of subway stops and kiosks, me alone in the streets while people in beds with goose down pillows were sleeping, caressed by gently humming summer fans in the electric night. Whoever said New York never sleeps was a fool. The city not only slept, it was in a coma, and I was stuck here, the only sentient thing in a relentless landscape of stone, metal, glass, asphalt, and dog shit. Even the few dusty specimens of plant life on Broadway seemed to have assumed the nature of quartz.

I was heading for Greenwich Village, too sober for comfort, when around 42nd Street this dude stood up from a covey of panhandlers. Engaged me with his eyes. Asked if I was a minister. Said I had the face of a minister and, well, he'd just gotten out of a shelter and was down on his luck. Used to be a pimp. Fancy cars, a mansion on Long Island with a five-car garage, and the women, you wouldn't believe all the women.

"Name is Leon," he says. "What's yours?"

After sixty blocks of sleeping Manhattan, the human contact was welcome. I shared my name and my troubles. When Leon found out I needed a place to stay, he was eager to help. Promised to show me somewhere to ride out the night. Sure, twenty bucks wasn't much, but he knew a place where I could get some shut-eye. So we walked through the neonlit jungle of signs for nudie shows, smells of popcorn and pine disinfectant, side-stepping the human wreckage on the sidewalk, indistinguishable from trash heaps till you saw movement, and there was a dim pair of eyes in the sooty face. I followed Leon around a corner, and he led me up some broken stairs. Above, there was an empty, overlit hallway that reeked cigarette smoke and Lysol. Hushed voices and strange sounds issued from behind closed doors.

Leon said he'd be right back and slipped around a fake wood-paneled corner.

Why didn't I just slip quietly down the stairs before Leon came back with a knife? But my feet wouldn't move, glued to the place where Leon left me. A few moments later he returned, deposited a shiny key in my palm with a wink, took my phony twenty-dollar bill in his hand, and was gone after telling me, "Room number eight." The key didn't fit in number eight, so I had to go down the hall and rouse the Rastafarian desk clerk to ask where my room was. He snored awake, and without any transition from sleep to wakefulness, he fended off my enquiries in a fierce language of scowls, shrieks and finger jabs, and then lay his head back on the counter and snored.

I'd been had. So had Leon.

My legs kept moving down Broadway, moving past Madison Square Garden, Union Square. The street numbers kept descending. I charted a course to Battery Park, hoping to gaze out over the dark waves to the Statue of Liberty raising her torch to Europe. The glow-in-dark numbers on my wristwatch showed around 4:30 a.m., and the wet, cool breeze augured a new day. In the confused and mazy streets by the Village I get turned around and somehow end up at the foot of the Brooklyn Bridge.

The East River glistened darkly against the shore lights. I breathed in the salt air from off the Atlantic and felt a breeze against my face. The author of *Look Homeward, Angel* used to come here to the foot of the Brooklyn Bridge after long bouts of writing on top of his refrigerator. To this very spot Thomas Wolfe came during the wee hours to gaze from the bridge over the dark waters and rest his eyes and weary soul.

There was a presence, a halo about the place.

"Well, Thomas, it's been quite a night," I said.

"What?! Someone talking to me?" a voice grumbled from the river.

"Yes," I uttered in dumb amazement.

"Thanks for remembering me. College professors don't like me much nowadays—all the empurpled prose and superlatives don't set well with all those Yankee professors. What really peeves me is how often I get confused with the other Wolf, the priggish fellow who wears the white suit."

Moisture came to my eyes, and I felt a prickling sensation on my scalp.

"Everything that's happened tonight could make some kind of story," said the river. "Hell of a story— specially the episode with Leon and the counterfeit bill."

"I was terrified, of course, but it all happened so fast."

"Living to tell the story is half the battle," said the river.

All was dark and silent as a tomb as I trudged back up Manhattan and eastward. Little by little the splendor of a new day showed over Central Park, and a whitish glow dawned over the lip of the horizon. Newspaper trucks started grumbling through the streets and ejected bales of papers. Columns of new sunlight crept up the sidewalks and they glittered with diamond-shards of glass and starry places where New Yorkers had spat. My ordeal was nearly over and my grateful feet quickened the pace.

On a streetcorner stood a girl in a satiny blue gown by one of the posh Central Park South hotels. Her presence, wreathed in a boa-like affair draped around her pale shoulders, was an event of the first magnitude in a street deserted as the moon. A chilly breeze of the coming day stirred the leaves of Central Park and stirred her semi-transparent skirt.

On the verge of passing her by, I saw a tear run down her face.

I turned and looked at her.

She had sea-blue eyes and hair the color of polished brass and very beautiful, smooth skin, and she was a little on the heavy side. She held her arms tightly around her chubby waist to keep from shivering.

"Looks like you had a rough night," she said in a Jersey slur.

"I've been out all night. I didn't have anywhere to stay."

"You could stay with me," she said.

"Look, I haven't got a cent. What's your name?"

"Sheila."

"Sheila, why do you think I spent all night walking?"

"What about your watch? It's a nice watch. Maybe we could make a deal and exchange your watch for—"

"Thanks anyway. I like to know what time it is."

"What, you don't like me? You think I'm too fat?"

"You're not fat."

"That awful word."

"I didn't say you're fat."

Her eyes puckered together and she made a high-pitched wailing sound.

"Don't cry, you're too beautiful to cry," I say, trying to leave her. Touching her shoulder in a parting gesture, I realized the goodness of her offer.

"I have a room where we can go," I said. "It won't be available for another hour."

"It's OK. You're kinda cute."

After a final detour to the United Nations plaza, the satiny waif and I reached Seventy-eighth and Lexington. Just that minute my host and a tall bony young woman bound from the doorway into the street. Both he and she were dressed for Wall Street. Trippler kissed Caitlin goodbye on tiptoes and turned away, brisk with aftershave, Brooks Brothers tie, sharkskin suit, highly polished shoes, and the smug smile of an easy conquest.

Sheila and I ensconced ourselves in a nearby doorway and waited for the former coxen of the Trinity rowing team to disappear down a subway entrance. Then we trudged upstairs, and I undressed and began to unzip her dress and massage her nipples. A phone ringing interrupted us. I sat up and crossed the room to get the phone. It was the chaplain of St. Paul's Chapel, on the Columbia campus; he had spoken to Mr. and Mrs. Powers, Mike's parents, in Memphis. Knowing I was in New York, they wanted me to speak at his memorial service that afternoon.

After the chaplain's call, my hard-on wilted. I fixed Sheila a cup of coffee. She told me about herself and looked at the window a lot. Her father was a refrigerator repairman, and she was working on her G.E.D. She didn't want to be a hooker all her life. I told her about the events of the last few days: coming to New York to see an old friend, and now I was going to deliver his eulogy.

"Just when I got here, this happened."

"You must feel awful," Sheila said.

"It's all too weird," I said.

"Nobody important in my life has died. I've got my grammy and grandpa. There was a hamster once that got out of its cage. My brother rolled over it and smothered it while he was sleeping."

"That's awful."

"You're here for a reason," she said. "God chose to put you here at this time and place."

Sheila looked out the window. I felt myself getting hard again and Sheila's hands started to explore me.

She left the apartment wearing my wristwatch. After a sweaty nap, I put on a shirt retrieved from the floor and took a cab to Morningside Heights. Standing before the gathering of friends and family in St. Paul's Chapel, furiously fanning themselves in the heat, I was infused by new energy. Sheila was right, there *was* a reason for my being here.

Talking to Mike's parents afterward and sharing their grief, I learned how Mike died. After a month's training in Abu Dhabi on the Persian Gulf, he started with the BCCI in Manhattan. Whatever the BCCI was, it sounded important.

The night I arrived in New York, Mike left his inhaler at the office, got home, and in the July heat of his stuffy, newly painted apartment suffered an asthma attack. His fiancée came to visit and, alarmed that Mike didn't answer the door, summoned the building super and they found him face-down on the floor. He'd been dead over an hour.

The day after Mike's memorial service, I got out of Dodge, headed west to California and a fresh start.

Time flowed on, but Mike Powers remained in my awareness. I found myself thinking about Mike sometimes with the sort of fixed saintly quality a person assumes when they cease to breathe, when they can no longer leave smudges on glass, or sneeze or snore or fart, surprise or exasperate. That was so untrue to Mike. It seemed pitifully unfair that his nemesis was absentmindedness—something as trivial an asthma inhaler forgotten at work one hot, hot August day in New York. It was a death unworthy of Hyperbolic Man.

One day, four or five years after Mike's death, I picked up the newspaper to see the baseball scores and stumbled on an article:

> The Bank of Commerce and Credit Inter-
> national, better known as BCCI, is entangled
> in what financial experts term the greatest
> banking scandal in world history. Yesterday
> the Bank of England issued orders to close

> the BCCI's branches in a dozen countries
> after discovering 9.5 billion dollars in assets
> missing.

My eyes read on:

> From Indian shopkeepers to entire third-
> world governments—all have entrusted their
> money to the BCCI, judging it safer than
> investing in their own unstable countries.
> China alone has more than $400 million
> invested in the bank headquartered in Abu
> Dhabi . . .

Abu Dhabi. My gaze riveted to the name. To tell you the truth, I always had my doubts the place existed, quite sure Abu Dhabi was one of the Hyperbolic Man's fabrications.

The newspaper got me thinking. I phoned Mr. and Mrs. Powers in Memphis.

"Did you see the news about the BCCI?"

"It's really something," Mike's mom said.

"Tell me, didn't the super in Mike's building say he was reaching out for a telephone?"

"Why yes, I think he did."

"I believe I've solved the riddle of Mike's death."

This was my gift to the Powers, concocting a superbly hyperbolic death for Mike, the Hyperbolic Man. The BCCI story provided the missing link to explain Mike Power's demise and cleanse away some of the unfairness. After all, according to the super in

Mike's building, he'd been found sprawled with his hand clawing air and, nearby, a telephone receiver off the hook.

He had known too much. And somebody in BCCI's New York offices had snatched his inhaler during lunch break, provoking his asthma attack. Mike Powers had known too much and in his last earthly seconds, reached out his hand for the telephone and meant to gasp out the words and blow the whistle that would bring down the whole venal charade.

"He was rubbed out," I said.

"Oh, that's wild," Mrs. Powers laughed. "Mike would have really loved that. You know how he adored that cloak and dagger stuff . . . So how are you doing, Jed?" Mrs. Powers asked.

"Great," I said. "I'm living in a big house with a view of the Hollywood sign."

"So, how are you doing?" she said. "Oh, I'm sorry, I already asked you that, I know. I'm so sorry."

"It's OK," I said. "I'm living in a big house, all right, but with a lot of weird people. All of us are in rehab."

"Gosh," she said, not knowing what to say. Telling some people you're in rehab is like admitting you're an axe-murderer.

After this yawning pause, Mrs. Powers surprised me and said something I'm still turning over. "Whatever you do, Mike is with us, helping us. And I'm sure he's going to help you, Jed. He's your angel. You can tell when he's in the room because your eyes water up, like when you slice onions, and there's a tingling breath from above, prickling on your scalp. It's because angels are so tall. Some are over eight feet tall, you know."

After drawing the conversation to a polite close, I hung up and looked around the dingy living room of the Twelve-Step house, located in an L.A. neighborhood I'd prefer my sister not visit. Strict curfew and no dope, no drink.

The black dude with curlers in his hair was drying his fingernail polish. He called herself Honey "Cuz I'm so sweet" and lived in a roomful of vitamins, vitamin jars on the table, on the chair, packing the shelves and spilling onto the floor. Honey is HIV+. The Honduran was mopping the kitchen floor with Pine-Sol for the fifth time this morning. Alberto moved into a twelve-step house because he caught himself drinking three beers every night after work—not enough to float a goldfish. Three. Lousy. Fucking. Beers.

The Czech dude coming off heroin was doing crosswords in the corner, humming to himself. Some nights Emil got the sweats and the liquid squeezed out of his bedsheets could fill two water glasses.

He said he made it a special point to eat in McDonalds in every country he visited to see what was different on the menu.

"In Norway they had lox on hamburger buns," he said. "In Athens you could get a Greek salad. There was chutney in India; I saw people put it on their fries. In Japan, I asked some guy where to get a really good meal in a fine restaurant. He told me how to get there, down so many blocks and to the right. I go there, afraid I may not be dressed right, and it's a freaking McDonalds . . . In China the menu was all the same: Big Macs and Coca-Cola. All the same. They had nothing different in China."

If I squint hard from the bungalow porch, I can barely make out the white, individual letters spelling Hollywood through the tawny layers of smog. W-O-O visible in a gap between raggedy palms and the stucco top of the Sunset Lanai apartments. At times the goofy sign appears tantalizingly close and, other times, so impossibly far, as the hills rearrange themselves in different baffling topographies. A couple blocks can make the difference between what seems a short stroll away and something forbiddingly remote as the summit of Kilimanjaro. Yet the sign is always there, playing hide-and-seek with we groundlings.

We are all seekers until we stop seeking, and my heels seek the top of the letter "H." And when I reach it, the Hyperbolic Man will be there waiting. *What took you so long?* he'll exclaim with a shit-eating grin from ear to ear. Emil and Honey will be tap-dancing in that tinsel Olympus and Alberto will be slumped over in a beer buzz, and Sheila, Leon and Thomas Wolfe will be there too, making Dixieland jazz and fanning their sweaty faces with their own enormous feathered wings. Angels, all of us.

Poison Pen

A strange and disturbing sight met Grace Hunter's eyes as she gazed out her bedroom window one sleepless night. A man was being taken feet first out of a Tudor-style half-timbered "cottage" on Crescent Drive, dappled by pale red and blue swiveling lights; the law had arrived in silence, as they always did in discreet Beverly Hills. If not for the glossy, tasseled Bally loafers with chamois-colored leather soles sticking out beneath, Grace would not have recognized the man as a man; a sheet already covered his face.

Then a sleek mulberry-colored Jaguar pulled into the drive. A platinum blond bolted out and ran to the sheeted stretcher. The sheet was drawn back. Deep sobs soon heaved the body of Audrey Van Husen; she kneeled on the dewy lawn. From her corner bedroom window, beside the Italianate mantelpiece, Mrs. Hunter observed the dead man's blue and white countenance, under coldly flashing police lights. The dead are reputed to wear peaceful expressions, perhaps thanks to the artistry of morticians; this man looked angry, he looked pissed off, he looked like he wanted to get off that stretcher and hit someone.

A gaggle of neighbors were brought out of their houses by the swiveling lights and the quiet commotion. Leaving her snoring husband on the other twin bed, Mrs. Hunter put on her embroidered silk slippers, her camel-hair Chesterfield over her pajamas and ventured into the chilly California night. Audrey Van Husen, her composure partly recovered, went off on tearful jags between questions. Two cops were reeling the hornet-yellow tape around the perimeter of the crime scene. Inside a whey-faced man with a breathing mask was in the entrance sifting a fine white dust over the curving balustrade inside the mansion.

"Looks like a lemming," muttered one cop to a short, rumpled man coming up the brick steps. He wore glasses awkwardly fixed with masking tape. His growth of beard was as bad as ever, a full set of luggage parked under his tired eyes.

"What makes you think so?" he said in a high, raspy voice.

"We had to break a window to get inside," said the first officer. "Van Husen was sprawled on the floor. All the windows were locked, the back door was locked."

"All the windows sealed shut?" repeated the short stubby man.

"And Van Husen was inside, dead as Elvis. Can I help you, ma'am?" the beefier of the two said to Grace

Hunter in a tone that preluded no help at all.

"Friend of the family."

"Friend of the family, my Italian ass," said the short man.

Martini was no stranger to her, having donated goods for many charity auctions and often providing the nitty gritty background of police work for her crime stories, written pseudonymously under the name G. Hunter, so no one would know she was a woman. Martini's loose tie displayed what cereal he'd eaten for breakfast, and he looked as if he needed a shave. Badly.

"Did you hear or see anything, Mrs. Hunter?" the detective asked.

"No. I just saw the police lights and came outside."

"Well then, I'm sorry to be rude, but you'll have to scram, Mrs. Hunter. I've got an investigation to conduct."

It was troubling that death had slipped so quietly and easily through the neighbors' locked doors, thought Mrs. Hunter, tramping back to their house in her embroidered silk slippers. A man had killed himself, and not she nor her daughter, Amy, nor her husband Brad had heard a blessed thing.

In the obituary section of the paper, Grace Hunter truly met their neighbor for the first time. The late Charles Poole Van Husen had been an investment banker. Caucasian, 63 years old, survived by his wife of twenty-some years, Audrey. She had been Van Husen's second wife. There were two children from a first marriage.

The newspaper said: "His wife reports that he had been recently depressed over financial problems. Investigators suspect that Van Husen took his own life."

Mrs. Hunter was on the way to an appointment at the hair salon on Rodeo Drive, and she saw a gardener pruning the magenta-colored bougainvillea.

"Good morning," she said. "You're new here. I haven't seen you before."

The tank-topped gardener slowly turned his head above a tattooed shoulder and raised the sharp pruning shears in a brown hand and looked flatly at Mrs. Hunter. Maybe he didn't understand English.

"Yes," he said. "Right on both counts."

He understood English.

"I haven't seen Mrs. Van Husen's Jag come in and out of the driveway."

With a rhythmic *chk-chk-chk*, the gardener continued his labor of severing vines from the bougainvillea bush, without looking around.

"She moved out. Nobody here."

"Who do you work for, if I may ask."

"The real estate company," he mumbled.

"Oh, they don't want the place to go to pot if it's on the market."

"Yeah, right."

Audrey Van Husen must have moved out at night or when Mrs. Hunter was tied up at one of her charity events. She never saw a trace of the moving vans or the boxes.

Widow. The label didn't fit the vivacious, Barbie type of woman, still a knockout at over 50. Thanks to the marvels of plastic surgery and aerobics, she could show off her suspiciously large breasts with skin-tight blouses. Tanned, blonde and shrill, she bossed around the gardener on the other side of the fence. "José, prune the roses, José wax the leaves, weed the garden." She fancied electric blue cowboy hats and slitted bell bottoms that opened revealing shapely dainty feet in her salmon-platinum high heels.

While the women got their hair coifed and permed at Cristophe, shouting over the sound of whinnying hair dryers, they mused about Charles Van Husen's demise.

Financial demons could drive a man to suicide. It had happened before in this august community. The men, when they could no longer support the brigades of dress designers, florists and plastic surgeons who made their wives' rarified world go round, saw no other way out. The end of the road was known to come in solitary suites in four-star hotels after downing a fistful of Nembutal in a lonely goodbye-to-all-that cocktail.

"It is a form of cowardice," said Mrs. Hunter in her light-honey accent. "I quite honestly think if they had their druthers, they'd whack their whole families."

"What a way to talk," their seatmates in the salon reproved.

"I remember the real-estate man, Jake Sullivan. When he was sentenced for tax evasion, he checked into the Embassy Suites, wrote letters to all his friends."

"And then he checked out for good," quipped one of the matrons.

In Sullivan's case, there were daughters, and shame for not having lived up to the mortifying American ideal of success. Mrs. Hunter thought about Charles Van Husen, a placid-enough-looking fellow, with grown kids, and she just didn't see it. But one could never know what demons lurked inside a Lacoste shirt.

Her curiosity aroused after the hair-salon colloquy, Mrs. Hunter located the real estate agent who was handling the Van Husen house. A perpetual smile rested on the real estate woman's barely seamed, tanned face, surely the product of a tanning salon. Her manicured fingers held a clipboard and she wore a woven hat that gave her a jaunty elegance. Mrs. Hunter guessed the woman's age anywhere between sixty and eighty, thanks to various cosmetic enhancements. Then she saw the gnarled and age-spotted hands, whose fingers supported a dazzling array of gold and jewels, and she put the woman's age closer to eighty.

The asking price for the Van Husen "cottage" was 1.8. Here that meant million. They walked into a living room, a sunken job with a beamed ceiling. Above loomed a dramatic balcony with whorled wooden railings. Romeo and Juliet could do their scene from here and have space left over for a barbecue.

Brand new carpeting had been laid in the living room. It imbued the room with the obnoxious smell of fresh resin. Perhaps bloodstained carpet was bad for the real estate business.

The real estate maven cooed about the five bedrooms, waxed loquacious about the ornamental shrubs around the swimming pool. She was positively eloquent when it came to the wrought-iron bars over the windows and the inviolable walls surrounding the place and the alarm system.

"This home has an infallible security system. You can feel completely safe living here," said the real estate maven.

"It's funny how someone could get killed in a place like this," said Mrs. Hunter.

Mrs. Hunter saw the real-estate woman's smile lose a few kilowatts.

"Yes," she admitted slowly, and clarified, "It was a suicide."

"An open and shut case, as they say . . . Somehow it keeps reminding me of a kitten that we brought to my father's office."

"Excuse me?" said the elderly agent.

"My father was a cotton broker in Memphis, and once my sister and I brought this kitten to his office. We left it in a shoebox and stepped outside a few minutes, locking the door. And when we came back to that windowless office. It was gone. We searched high and low. In the bookshelves and on the floor. In drawers and on shelves. And when we came to grips that the tabby cat had gone for good, it emerged with a loud meow from a chair pushed under a desk. Nobody had ever thought of looking there."

They went downstairs from the kitchen to take a

look at the wine cellar, a feature that the real estate woman mentioned with slightly less enthusiasm than when pointing out the house's previous attributes. The cellar was uncobwebbed and tidy, and a few dusty vintages remained in the grooved spaces for the bottlenecks.

"Your name is Grace Hunter?" the real estate woman asked. "Say, you wouldn't be G. Hunter, who writes mystery stories."

"Why, to tell you the truth, I am," said Mrs. Hunter, flattered.

"You should be ashamed of yourself, giving people the idea murder is an everyday occurrence in Beverly Hills. It affects property values. And there is something so . . . unladylike about murder . . ."

"It does happen from time to time. Remember Johnny Stompanato and Bugsy Siegal met unfortunate ends in our lovely community."

"You know, my daughter went to school with Lana Turner's daughter. She's the one who got tired of Stompanato beating up on her mom and she stuck him with a kitchen knife. Served him right. If somebody were beating up on your mother—"

"Is there an attic?" Mrs. Hunter cut short the real-estate woman's murderous musings.

"Why, I believe so. I've never really looked."

"Shall we . . . ?"

They opened all the doors and closets of the upstairs bedroom. In the master bedroom, which had a raised platform for the bed, reached under Spanish arches, they opened a walk-in closet, at the far end of birdseye maple doors rose the hardwood rungs. Mrs. Hunter gave a sly look and began the difficult feat of scaling the rungs in high-heels. With surprising nimbleness, the elderly real estate woman followed close behind.

Into a dusky attic the two women emerged. Planks covered the rafters, exposed below were tongue-and-groove boards spewing plaster. The attic was dank, airless, and old smelling. The roof slanted down and neither of the two women could stand up.

"Watch your step," said the elderly real estate agent, staring up from a cramped position, "or you could end up in a heap of plaster on the floor of the upstairs bedroom."

Motes of dust floated alive in the beams of light that came through little porthole windows at the end of each gable.

"That gable on the far end has a window. I've seen it from outside," said Mrs. Hunter. "That's odd. Yet no light seems to be getting in."

"We really shouldn't be up here," said the real estate woman.

Mrs. Hunter approached what looked to be a solid partition of wood and rafters. Just what the police flashlights would have seen if they had come searching up here the night Charles Van Husen died. What Mrs. Hunter noted was a gap between the roofline and the wood below; it was a gap big enough to put her pinkie in and it was edged by light. At her touch the partition moved ever so slightly. At a push of the heel of her palm, the whole thing moved, revealing a crawl space about six feet long and two yards high at the apex. Light from the porthole window on the end of the gable exposed the scene: the floorboards were free of dust, compared to the rest of the attic, and cluttered by debris between the rafters. An ashtray overflowed with stubbed cigarette butts; a shred of newspaper that had words printed in Spanish, and an empty beer bottle, a cheap American brand.

"Oh my," gasped Mrs. Hunter.

"There's garbage up here," yelped the real estate woman, starting to reach for it.

"No, don't touch anything. It's evidence."

Detective Martini of the Beverly Hills police did not have to wait for Mrs. Hunter to pay him a visit. He was immediately summoned to the half-timbered mansion in the 900 block of Crescent Drive.

Mrs. Hunter triumphantly presented the findings of her real-life sleuthing. While being shown around by the real estate woman, she had discovered the secret compartment hidden by a plywood panel. She pointed proudly to the beer bottle and ashtray.

"Somebody was hiding up here," Martini said in his high-pitched, raspy voice. His slight stature enabled him the luxury of standing up to full height in the attic.

"The person who was living up here could have killed Charles Van Husen." Martini sighed when she said that. "Aren't you the slightest bit interested in finding the truth of what happened that night?"

"The truth," pronounced Martini, "is something lying at the bottom of a bottomless pit. I'm just here to find out who's guilty. Van Husen's wife was already investigated and cleared. She has an alibi; she was at a restaurant on Melrose the night of the suicide."

"Did they ever find a suicide note?"

"No," said Martini.

"How did the police come upon the locked house with a body inside?"

"A neighbor heard a gunshot and called 911."

"Maybe you should investigate who that neighbor was. Somebody wanted to call attention to the perfect suicide."

"And you think they did it?"

"I think there's more than meets the eye."

"You know, Grace, I think you're getting carried away by your writer's imagination. Oh yes, there's one other thing," he said. "Gunpowder tests were done on Van Husen's hands and he'd recently fired a pistol." After a pause Martini said, "As my granny from Palermo used to say, let sleeping dogs lie."

"Admit it, you're lazy," said Mrs. Hunter. "My Detective Marx would never take something like this lying down."

"I'm sorry I can't live up to your fictional hero. He's also six-foot-three and wears 700-dollar suits. Listen, why don't you go and write a story about the Van Husen business," Martini said. "You can write any cockamamie thing you want. I deal in facts."

Down the hill a stream of shimmering traffic went east-west on Sunset Boulevard and a tangerine-colored sunset set in over Century City. Just another day of lonely drivers, bedraggled women smoking distractedly, men in tawdry-trendy suits talking on cellphones. And Grace Hunter, it seemed, was alone in all the world, in caring about what might really have happened to Charles Van Husen.

The bitter legacy of this realization was assuaged in time by a new story.

Many writers say the trick is to write every day, but Mrs. Hunter was just the opposite. "I'm a writer three days out of the month," she often said. An idea seized her imagination and she could pour it out on the laptop in one sitting. That's how it was with "Open and Shut," a tale so shamelessly inspired by the Van Husen case, it practically had Audrey Van Husen's fingerprints on it, begun on a Tuesday and mailed to *Murder Digest* the following Friday. She wasn't sure that they'd buy the ruse of the husband being shot after his Wednesday session at a basement shooting range, so that gunpowder tests would prove positive and they'd rule it a suicide, but what the heck. What the heck, she thought, slipping the envelope bound for New York into the mailbox.

Afterward, G. Hunter became Mrs. Hunter again, and her energies were channeled into handling the adolescent hysterics of her daughter Amy and preparing a charity fundraiser, "Drills on Wheels," a mobile dentistry unit for impoverished inner city children. It came off without a hitch in the rose-and-gold ballroom of the Beverly Hills Hotel and was a star-studded success. Madonna's lingerie went for a cool hundred thousand. Somebody bid 20,000 dollars to do lunch with her powerful producer husband; then a former partner of Brad's bid 20,000 *not* to do lunch with him.

In all, the women of Beverly Hills fleeced the rich and famous to the tune of a couple million to prevent tooth decay in the needy children in the South Central ghetto.

After the charity ball, the old boredom set in. Outsiders wouldn't believe it, but there was plenty to be bored about in Beverly Hills. The suntanned phonies and the stream of predictable charity-event-filled days grew stale after a while. The dazzling sunshine and symmetrical rows of palm trees skewering the horizon lost their charm. It got tiresome turning away the occasional tourist, duped by an out-of-date map of the stars' homes he'd just paid six bucks for, buzzing on the intercom and looking for a movie star who'd lived here thirty years ago.

December became May, and still no word from *Murder Digest* about Mrs. Hunter's story. She surmised that its twist, involving a staged suicide the same day the husband went to an indoor shooting range, had been too much for the editor to swallow. Oh well. In defiance she printed out a new copy and mailed it to *The New Yorker.*

Meanwhile, Mrs. Hunter's producer husband, Brad, accompanied his latest celluloid extravaganza to Cannes. Mrs. Hunter had not wanted to go: "It's always the same people, the same false smiles, the same old jeweled bitties, cinema fags and blown-dry producers second-guessing the jury. And you still can't get away from the palm trees."

Rather, she wanted to stay in Beverly Hills and start a new crime story, the latest adventure of her fictional detective Marx. In the end, though, she ceded to the lure of travel, for new places, sights, and smells always fueled a writer's imagination.

Brad and she got off the airplane and were whisked away in a monstrous white SUV. They wound down a ribbon of highway and over the cusp of a range of green and blue mountains, on the other side huddled villas and bleached white cottages fringed the azure sea.

That afternoon, before the first festival screening, the festival guests were sunning their bodies in chaise-longues around a pool, whose silvery reflections darted across their faces. A candy-striped umbrella protected Mr. and Mrs. Hunter from the blazing sun. Brad was chain-smoking, nervous about audience reaction to his new flick. Behind the cover afforded by his Hollywood magnate sunglasses, his eyes would move from side as some neon-bikinied babe moved her tanned hips along the pool's edge.

"Look at that table on the other side of the pool," exclaimed Mrs. Hunter. "Don't they look familiar? I wonder what movie I've seen them in."

Brad scooted his sunglasses down his nose to see them. Nine times out of ten his wife was right about recollecting faces seen in movies.

He saw a well-preserved blond talking animatedly into a cellphone. She wore humongous sun-glasses that covered half her face. A one-piece, zebra-stripe swimsuit covered her aerobic-toned body. She hung up the telephone and kissed her companion on the cheek. The cheek belonged to a handsome Mexican face with very bright yet sleepy brown eyes.

Mrs. Hunter had seen that face before, too, and those sun-darkened arms hosing down walkways, handling garden shears.

"I don't remember seeing them in any movie."

"That's Audrey Van Husen," Grace said *sotto voce*. "And that's the Van Husen's old gardener."

Mrs. Hunter immediately bustled herself over to the table and gushed, "Audrey, dear, what a surprise!"

"How have you been," said the blond. "I'm sorry I . . ."

"Oh, you don't remember me. I'm Grace Hunter—your old neighbor in Beverly Hills."

"Wow. Small world," the blond gushed with a vacant stare.

"My husband brought a film down to the festival."

"What film is that?"

"He says it's a cross between *Star Wars* and *Shakespeare in Love*. Designed to please all audiences."

"What's it called?"

"I'm sorry I don't know. I try to know as little about

my husband's films as possible. Long ago I put our marriage before my husband's career and have refrained from critical comment about his projects. Tell me, what have you been doing with yourself?" she said with a show of Beverly Hills hypocrisy, "You look divine."

"This is paradise. I'm living here in a villa called *Mon Paradis*, and the help is cheap. We have a cook, two cleaning ladies and a gardener for a song."

"I see you have a gardener," Mrs. Hunter commented archly.

A queasy look passed over Audrey's face; she flushed.

"This is Fernando," she said. Mrs. Hunter extended a hand to the Mexican stripling a fraction of Audrey Van Husen's age. A smile of dazzling whiteness drenched his nutmeg-colored face. When Mrs. Hunter left them alone, he went back to his job of rubbing coconut oil over Audrey Van Husen's freckled shoulders in the hot Mediterranean sun.

The festival passed, as festivals do, between a whirlwind of cocktail parties and screenings. Brad Hunter got suddenly called back to Hollywood early. His latest production was in dire need of his presence. It was already several million over budget and an actress had stormed off the set. He flew back to Los Angeles and left Grace alone in Cannes.

The last night of the festival, Grace went to a party at *Mon Paradis*, the showplace home of Audrey Van

Husen, perched high on a mountain, commanding a view of Monaco. The moon was a slice of lemon. The guests clinked glasses under Chinese lanterns that bobbed in the ocean breeze. There were more tuxedos at the black-tie affair than at a high school senior prom, and the "young things" wore audaciously low-cut scintillating gowns and diamonds on their shriveled necks that gleamed like the studded lights on the shore of Montecarlo.

Audrey was attended by her young lover. They were like a couple of teenagers shoving paté in each other's mouths and laughing under the canopy of night.

During the festivities Mrs. Hunter and her scotch strayed off into Audrey's study and her eyes ranged over the books, mostly shallow bestsellers in keeping with Audrey's shallow character. On one side table she saw the latest *New Yorker*. In the table of contents she saw a story by G. Hunter. It magically opened right to the page where the tale began:

> *A sleek Jaguar pulled into the drive as a man was being taken feet first from a Tudor-style half-timbered "cottage" on Crescent Drive. No observer would have identified him as a man if it weren't for his glossy, tasseled Bally loafers with chamois-colored leather soles sticking out beneath; a sheet already covered his face . . .*

The way the magazine opened right to her story, Audrey Van Husen must have read her story, Mrs.

Hunter deduced. The pleasant shock of seeing her words in print was tempered by sudden embarrassment.

What would Audrey think? After the splendid way she had been treated by her hostess, Grace felt ashamed of how she had lampooned Audrey in "Open and Shut."

It grew late, and yawns came easily to Mrs. Hunter's lips; she had an early flight to catch to Los Angeles. Audrey was alone on the terrace, bringing a glass of champagne to her rouged lips. The petting party had ended and Fernando seemed to have drifted off to bed.

"Dear, you look tired," Audrey said to Mrs. Hunter. "Take a taxi to the hotel. Let me call you a car."

Audrey accompanied her down a graceful flight of marble steps to a waiting stretch limo.

The limo lurched into gear and the dark highway tumbled past, and Mrs. Hunter felt a twinge of regret for not asking Audrey's opinion of her story. Then her mind could be at rest, and she could enjoy a few hours of untroubled sleep before going to the airport.

An awning of twined tree branches arched overhead, as they neared the turn-off to the hotel, but the driver didn't turn off the highway. He kept barreling around the curves and down the road to Montecarlo.

"You missed the turn," Mrs. Hunter said. "The hotel's back there."

The silent figure, behind a glass partition, made no noise.

"Where are we going?" Mrs. Hunter said in passable French. The silent figure in the front seat still made no reply. "Tell me, please. Where're we going?" her voice became shriller.

She tried roll down a window, but the handle broke off in her hand. She tried to undo the locks in the back doors; she found only thin screw that her fingers couldn't grasp and one of her nails broke. What kind of limo was this? Then the figure in the front seat turned around and bestowed a smile on her that chilled her to the marrow. She recognized the chiseled profile of Fernando.

"You were right," he said over the intercom. His sharp little incisors gleamed in the moonlight. "How did you know we planned the murder to occur the same day Charles Van Husen went to the shooting range?"

"Intuition, I guess," replied Mrs. Hunter coolly, and in one deft motion her hand reached for the cellphone in her evening bag. She punched the long foreign code into the phone and waited for Brad or her daughter Amy to answer. Behind the glass, she saw Fernando's face lose its smugness, and a grimness set in.

Finally there was an answer. Her daughter was home. Thank God.

"Amy," said Grace.

"No, this isn't Amy. Who's this?" said a high, little-girl voice on the other end.

"Is Brad Hunter there?"

"Brad isn't here," replied a bimbo's vacant falsetto. "He said never answer the phone, but I heard it ringing so many times, I thought it might be something important . . . Who is this?"

Now as Mrs. Hunter sat in the back seat of the limousine, she heard Detective Martini's high, raspy voice telling her, "Truth is something lying at the bottom of a bottomless pit."

Now she knew the truth, incontrovertibly; truth's cold embrace held her as the long car hurtled toward oblivion.

Fitzroy

A man, attired in a business suit the color of ashes, came out into the populous street in the small Mexican town, radiating the confidence that emanated from having made a new bet in the casino of life. He had just bought his weekly lottery ticket. Although he wore a business suit, he was not, strictly speaking, a member of their entrepreneurial tribe—he fancied himself a psychologist and that is what he would have emblazoned on his business card. Somehow, though, he never got around to printing the cards up because he had trouble settling on one name.

His tall, slightly stooped figure strolled down Avenida Madero when he spied a gentleman among the clusters of people in the plaza. Friendly blue eyes fastened on him. Slow recognition. Then he saw the un-oiled wheels turn in the head of the old legionnaire and his mouth began to work.

"Where's my money?" the legionnaire spat out.

Before the man in the suit could summon a response, the old man rose toward him with the speed of a teenager, and snorted:

"Listen, Murphy, you promised that as soon as you got back to Chicago, you were going to send me a check. Where's my goddamn money? And what the hell are you doing here when you're supposed to be in Chicago."

"Mergers and acquisitions."

"And your hair . . . it was black and now it's red."

"I'm so sorry. My secretary must have dropped the ball," he said. "I left detailed instructions with your address for the check to be sent by express mail."

"Express? It's been two months."

"Two months!" the man replied. "I'm gonna call my secretary."

He punched a series of numbers into his cellphone, betraying his disgust with the delay.

"Hello," he spoke into the phone. "This is Grant Murphy. Connect me with Linda," after a pause, a sharpness emerged in his voice, "This is Grant and I'm with Al Snyder and he's asking me what happened with his check. What's going on here? I already thought that. No way . . . Christ, this poor man has waited patiently for his check for months . . . Please, Linda, don't let this happen again. Or you're going to want to polish up your resume . . ."

A brusque hand movement ended the call.

He turned to the gentleman, the former commander of American Legion Post 9, who had a strong jaw, a beer belly girdled by Sansabelt slacks.

"I'm so ashamed. It seems there was a mistake on the part of my secretary."

"How are you going to pay me?"

"Let me make it up to you," the man said. "We'll go in my taxi to the Hotel Monte Carlo, a couple blocks from here, and I'll pay you in cash."

"Wait a hot second, Mr. Fast Talker. I want to see your cellphone."

Before he could say anything, the old man's brown, bony hand grabbed it.

"Aha!" he exclaimed. "It's a toy. Not even a real cellphone. You know what you are, you're a fake! I want my money."

The man began to run through the populous street in Chapala, chased by the furious legionnaire.

Like the migrating birds, each spring he left Guadalajara for Mazatlán in order to avoid the rains. The rainy season was depressing as the smell of old coffee and reminded him of New York winters. From Mazatlán he'd journey to Puerto Vallarta when the broiling dog days ebbed. From there to the lakeshore of Chapala for winter.

For work he wore a worsted wool suit that had seen

better days and a power-red necktie. A scuffed leather briefcase completed the uniform. More than once a shoeshiner had facetiously volunteered to shine his briefcase. In such business attire, he never lacked for generous-hearted gringos who would open their hearts when hearing his woeful traveler's tale. The tale was always the same, more or less: he'd change cities, New York, Chicago or San Francisco. Sometimes he had a wife, sometimes he was divorced.

"You're American! Oh my God, I'm so happy to know someone who speaks English," he'd gush out, hyperventilating. "I was on my way to the airport and we stopped in a taxi. I got out to break a hundred-peso bill for the taxi driver, and the instant I turned my back, the driver drove off with my camera, wallet, suitcases. Everything."

"Terrible," the listener would say or something of the sort.

"My plane leaves at seven. I have twenty minutes to get to the airport."

"I'll be happy to give you a lift," the good Samaritan might say.

"Oh, no no no no. That would be asking too much, but if you could help, any amount however small would be appreciated. I'll pay you the minute I get back to Chicago. In fact, I'm going to call my secretary." He'd take out his toy phone and was the very picture of a lawyer who worked in corporate mergers.

Thanks to the gringos' generosity, he always emerged from these encounters a little richer. Often a *lot* richer, on occasion enough for three months rent because the gringos like to show off the size of their hearts. They were his bread and butter.

But today had been a day without butter and without bread. The landlady was pressuring him for the rent, and he had to do something soon. He was hungry. He knew he was the owner of a winning lottery ticket, but he still could have bought a sandwich instead of a ticket. To make matters worse, the old legionnaire had recognized him; coloring his thatch of hair hadn't been enough to hide his distinctive features: hawk eyes and a large beak nose. Now in the heat of the hunt, Snyder the legionnaire was flanked by two policemen, who ran down the street. Murphy slipped into an open shop doorway and became fascinated by a bead necklace. He breathed relief when he saw Snyder and the two policemen go by. Immediately he left the doorway and went the opposite way.

In the corner store a pleasant American woman heard the short version of the lawyer's tale.

"What thieves," she said. "They see Americans here and they take advantage. We have always to be on our toes, Mr. O'Connor," said the woman, peeling off a hundred dollar bill.

In Guadalajara, some forty minutes later, he walked among the downtown throngs, through the plazas and past the cathedral. The hawk eye detected some gringos, students abroad, shorts and backpack, but he couldn't connect with them. He needed mature (i.e. borderline senile) gringos to establish rapport, for they were blinded by his aplomb and immaculate laundering, blinded to the seediness that sabotaged his carefully cultivated professional image: tiny stains on his necktie, a missing button on his suit, a spot of dried shaving cream on his cheek where he missed shaving.

Economizing, he took a bus for a few centavos to an American-style mall. As the crowded bus sped up the avenue he held onto a railing with his right hand and his left periodically checked to see that no pickpocket had visited. The sooty bus screeched to a halt and he got off at Plaza del Sol. There he spied a woman, advanced in years but still handsome, waiting at the edge of the sidewalk. Her impeccably blond hair was pulled up, a parti-colored silk scarf was looped with just the right nonchalance around her neck, and she waited. Her gloved hands tightly held a fine handbag.

"You're American," he began.

She turned and said yes with no particular enthusiasm.

"My God, what I thrill to find someone who speaks English," he said, toning it down somewhat. The refined presence of this woman had already begun to work in him. "I'm a lawyer from New York and you won't believe what just happened to me. I was heading to the airport in a taxi and we stopped at a liquor store so I could change a hundred-peso bill to pay the driver."

"Oh, isn't it a nuisance! They never have change."

"I turned my back and the guy, pardon me, the taxi driver drove off with my suitcases, money, everything. And now my flight leaves in twenty minutes."

"Mister . . . ?

"Fitzroy."

"You'll have to excuse me," the woman said. "I'm terrible with names."

"Me too. They never stick to me for long."

"Well, Mr. Fitzgerald, forgive me, Fitzroy. Why don't you call the airline and change your reservation? You'll never reach the airport in 20 minutes . . . Oh, I'm so sorry," she extended a petite hand gloved in fine thin leather and held him in her almond eyes, "I'm Nora Cavanaugh. Now Mr. Fitzroy, please be a darling and be our guest at Villa de las Palomas. We're having a party tonight after the opera. Tell me," she looked at him enquiringly with her almond eyes, "Are you one of the Fitzroys from Palm Beach?"

"We're the Fitzroys from Hell's Kitchen, New York."

There slowly pulled up to the curb a long car with Mrs. Cavanaugh's driver and Fitzroy climbed docilely into the back seat.

Palm Beach, Cap Ferrat, the Côte d'Azur in France . . . the heiress Nora Cavanaugh had always been partial to glamorous places. Guadalajara sort of broke the magical chain of names. For one thing, it was as far inland as she had ever lived and yet here she had been able to create a world all her own that sustained her dearest illusions. She lived in a French provincial mansion surrounded by Lombardy poplars. When Mrs. Cavanaugh's car came to the gates of the Villa de las Palomas, they still had more than three minutes in the car to reach the main house. Nora's guest, known to her as Mr. Fitzroy, couldn't believe this oasis of luxury in the middle of Mexico, he thought as he lounged in a king-size bed in a wing for Mrs. Cavanaugh's guests. Marvelous. An unprepossessing man in a guayabera shirt knocked softly on the door and brought Fitzroy a silk dressing gown and a bottle of single-malt whisky.

"I hope the gown fits. If it doesn't I can take care of it for you," the man said in precise English, perfectly measured as Sinatra's pauses

"One size fits all," Fitzroy said leering at the bottle. The manservant chuckled mutely.

"Mrs. Cavanaugh would like to know if you will be attending the opera."

"No thank you," he replied with a small bow as his graciousness continued to blossom. "I have to stay up and study legal documents." And then it occurred to him that he didn't have to explain anything to anybody, as he was used to doing with old legionnaires and retirees. He had already made the sale to Mrs. Cavanaugh: look at this place, paneled walls and foam-green carpet under his feet. Besides an ordinary commode, there was a very funny device in the bathroom: water fountained up in the middle of the porcelain bowl where there should have been a drain. This was a whole new world.

Frankly, his presence at the opera would also expose

him needlessly to the ire of former "clients" who had been taken in by his story and there could be an unpleasant scene. Better to bathe himself, dwelling in the aroma of perfumed bathing salts, put on his silk robe and bask in the splendor of Villa de las Palomas. He contemplated his lottery ticket with sweetness in the rosy-gold radiance of the setting sun. Later he fell sound asleep and dreamed that he was underneath a cement mixer truck that tilted up and out poured bills, more and more bills on top of him. He danced like a madman under the green cascade.

The music woke him up. There were strains of 'La Traviata' and the soprano who had been Madame Butterfly that night sang alongside a bearded baritone. He stepped up to the balcony window. By night Villa de las Palomas presented a grander spectacle than by day. Lights illuminated the trees and circular fountains of carved rose-colored stone sang.

Already dressed in his newly pressed lawyer's suit, he went downstairs. Mid-staircase, he was suddenly overwhelmed by the deep conviction that this was the greatest party ever. The most stunning women, the most gorgeous jewels, and the handsomest men in tuxedos, gathered round a Steinway piano twelve-feet long. And the soprano and baritone were holding that last long note of a duet, and their bodies went slack when the note ceased and they drank in vigorous applause.

"Nora always has the most fabulous parties," said a man with an ascot tie. Outside of movies Fitzroy had never seen a living soul wear an ascot. "There's always a surprise around the corner."

The guest savored flaky pastry crowns filled with smoked salmon and pimento, and the wine goblet always stayed at the same level no matter how much he drank. Fitzroy strolled around, breathing in a rare, expendable perfume, and he sat spellbound at one of the poolside tables, where countless romances were being born. Any of these beauties, he realized with a thrill, could help him get the honest job of being a kept man. Fitzroy met a professional polo player from Argentina. He had never dreamed in all his days that he would meet a polo player.

Heedless of the hour—it was well past midnight—Mrs. Cavanaugh phoned her administrator. Hastings was a tired man with large bags under his eyes, a somber man, who had accompanied Nora from the time of her wild youth in New York, to Cap Ferrat, Palm Beach and Palm Springs, through various marriages with gold-diggers, gigolos, and one good man, and finally he had come with her to Villa de las Palomas. Though he had always been there for her, there were many things she did not know about Hastings, like his first name. She thought nothing of calling him at three in the morning and dragging him out of bed.

"Hastings, the party has to go on. Be a darling, and bring a case of champagne."

"Yes, madam," he said humbly.

The party continued its mad career. The polo player fell half naked into the pool. The champagne ran out.

"Where is Hastings? Why is he taking so long?" Mrs. Cavanaugh asked.

Then there was a commotion. Hastings entered, his manner grave, with two servants scampering after and holding two boxes aloft. The clumps of revelers made way for the new arrival.

"Here is the champagne, madam," said the administrator. "Two cases of Dom Perignon. That is all, madam."

"I only asked for one. That was so nice of you. You know me so well." He nodded his head. "And how on earth did you find Dom Perignon on such short notice."

"I have had these for quite some time," he said and gazed at her. His face seemed to relax, the bags under his eyes dissolved, and a surprising gleam came into his eye. "For years I warned you about squandering money," Hastings said. "Fabulous parties and chauffeurs. It was a last resort that you move to this savage provincial city where it was possible to sustain the luxury to which you are accustomed."

The guests were suddenly looking perplexed.

"But now there is the inescapable moment of truth," the administrator continued. "You have never listened to old Hastings, but to high-society mavens who accelerated your ruin."

"They know how to have a good time," she said.

"That's the first topic that should taught in school, Hastings. To have a good time. I don't know why they bother with all that math and numbers."

"All these parties," he made a dismissive gesture with his hands. "The frivolity."

The revelers looked on, flabbergasted.

"We have spent the last cent. There is nothing left," Hastings said in a brittle voice. "I won't be needing these any more, since there's nothing left to administer," he handed her a large metal ring, jammed by keys.

All the revelers stood gaping, all except the polo player who watched, half submerged, at the pool's edge. The opera singers' sunny faces became pinched.

"It does no good to cry," Mrs. Cavanaugh said. "A toast!" The servants uncorked the bottles. "You too, stuffy old Hastings."

All the servants who'd be on the street, looking for a job the next day, filled with glasses with brio.

"Good times," they toasted, "good times."

Fitzroy was stunned by the series of events. All the glittering wealth melted like candle wax before his eyes, dissolved as sand-castle turrets buffeted by waves.

Then the polo player drunkenly shouted:

"Nora, you are fabulous. Stop it! Stop it!" he started laughing. "Shamelessly pulling our leg this way."

The soprano from the opera looked at him and started to giggle. In turn the man with the ascot let out a huge booming laugh, spilling his drink all over himself. A servant or two joined in. Soon the whole room resounded with cackles and belly laughs, a perfect storm of laughter that made the chandelier crystals tremble. In spite of himself old Hastings cracked a smile.

"How precious, what a precious practical joke," said the opera baritone.

Mrs. Cavanaugh smiled indulgently and her administrator toasted. "Thank you, Hastings. This has been most delicious."

"You really outdid yourself this time," said dour Hastings.

"Cheers to you," said Mrs, Cavanaugh, "and long live the party!"

The revelers broke up again into couples and small groups. The Dom Perignon poured from bottle after bottle. The man in the recently pressed business suit (still frayed though a missing button had been replaced) knew how to read people; it was his bread and butter. He knew that Nora Cavanaugh was as broke as he had been this afternoon in Chapala. The new lottery ticket crinkled in the darkness of his pocket. He felt its smooth surface rub between his fingers, then he extracted it and looked at it lovingly, sure that it was a winner.

"Nora," he said tentatively, "I want to give this to you for being so kind to me. It's a lottery ticket. Results are announced on Wednesday."

"Oh, thank you, Mr. Fitzroy. Wednesday always was my lucky day," she said grasping the ticket. Then it flew from between her fingers.

Fitzroy, gentleman that he'd become, bent down despite his bad back and picked it up.

For one fleeting instant he thought of keeping the ticket for himself, but a noble urge got the better of him, and he handed Nora the ticket. He liked being Fitzroy. Maybe he'd finally print up those business cards.

American Paranoia

Once . . . twice . . . three times . . . now five . . . the phone rings, a grinding tinkle in the silent, thick darkness before dawn. Your hand and fingers reach defiantly for the receiver and then stutter in midair before picking it up. Should you? It's not for you, the call is for another man: you're not even supposed to be here. You're an intruder. Silence circles the phone and blankets the room while a supersonic hum, audible only to canine ears, spreads outward. In a hidden patio a rooster clucks, preliminary to crowing. As doubt fades away, replaced by eddying waves of a quixotic comfort, the ringing starts up again. Should you or shouldn't you? Let's put an end to this game, pick up the damn thing.

"Yes . . ." *noncommittal, unsure who you should be. Wrong man in the wrong place.*

"Good morning," *peals out a smiling Mexican woman.*

"Your wake up call, mistair."

You chuckle to yourself and fumblingly replace the receiver on the cradle, begin again the pilgrimage back toward peace and quiet. Again the phone rings.

"Yeah, hello . . ."

"Señor Poindexter," *says a hard male voice in the receiver, remote and tinny on a faraway line riddled by ghosts and echoes of trans-Atlantic conversations, overlapped and melted into one dirge of hysterical cries and lunatic laughter that conveys the collective wail of humanity.* "Did you do the job?"

"Sí," *you answer diffidently, masking raw nerves.*

"Muy bien," *the suave voice approves. The sudden shade of warmth, intruding in the gravelly voice, sends a chill up your weary spine.* "Are you satisfied?"

"Totalmente," *you respond, gringo-accented. Your muscles ache and a satisfied weariness rises in your bones. Killing is hard work. You wait for the faraway voice to speak again, you want it to speak and obliterate the madhouse chirps and laughter, coughs and cries of* "no no no" *in the fuzzy void.*

"That little key we gave you," *its brass gleams dully on the nightstand.* "Take that to safe-deposit box 983 at the South Beach branch of the Miami First National Bank. Your payment will be waiting."

After a pause you venture, "Is it the amount we agreed upon?" *Breaking day silvers a bed and bureau. You shudder, seeing that the espresso stains on your buff-colored poplin trousers are the rust color of dried blood.*

"Yes," *says the cold voice,* "fifty thousand cash."

♦ ♦ ♦

She was a blond men drooled over, and a few women too. Boys had used every trick in the book to coax her phone number out of her. Lewd uncles had pawed her milky thighs, took her home in a mind's eye snapshot, disrobed her and twitched in bed with their wives, thinking about her. But that was back when love beads were the rage and Nixon had an address on Pennsylvania Avenue, and the Viet Kong blew up in my face . . .

Now a sun-dried prune of a sex kitten gazed at me from across my dusty desk.

"Gracias, Señor Santana," the prune said to my offer of a wobbly chair.

"You can use English," I said. "Call me Tony."

"Tony . . ."

I wondered if she was always that easy to boss around, and lit up a Delicado.

"You have taken on a case recently . . ." she said in a creamy English accent.

I blew smoke down my chin. The long strands of smoke drifted lazily across the window, specked by dust and last summer's raindrops. In the thronged plaza below, two fat brown men in red suits and white beards competed for the kiddies to have their photo taken with one of them. Confronted by dueling Santas, a youngster began to bawl to Mommy. The ratty burro with fake reindeer antlers strapped on its head looked on with huge, sad eyes.

"Could you please not blow smoke in my face, Mr. Santana."

"I was gonna offer you a cigarette . . . A drink?"

"No thanks. José Cuervo and I are divorced," she said with a curt nod of her ash blond head, "What's that?" she pointed to the tarnished medal hanging on the wall from a faded gold-fringed purple ribbon.

"Nothing you want to hear about," I said and tried to blow my smoke away from her. "I'm sorry, ma'am. I didn't catch your name?"

"I didn't say it." She testily adjusted leathery hands over a purse in her lap.

A weak smile dribbled out the corners of my mouth.

"I'm Lady Carolyn Carlisle-Watts. You know my son, Tristan," she said. It wasn't a question. "He asked you to look into the circumstances surrounding the death of my late husband, John Watts. Mr. Santana, I would like you to please discontinue your investigation."

This got me up from my sleepy slouch.

"I'm willing to pay your usual fee, and a little extra," she said. "You may wonder why it's so important for me that you drop this case. Number one, this obsession with his father's death is beginning to affect Tristan's medical studies; his grades are slipping. He'd applied to over 20 medical schools in the U.S. It was a miracle he got accepted into Guadalajara. Also, after being through the grieving process myself for so many, many years, it is no picnic to dredge this thing up . . . I believe in letting sleeping dogs lie."

"So do I . . ."

"I can see that. You don't want to talk about your Purple Heart."

Lady Carolyn got out her checkbook. I watched her slender fingers curl around a Mont Blanc pen and swirl her signature. She gracefully waved the signature dry and handed me the check. It was all too beautiful to interrupt.

"I'm sorry, but I have to ask you for cash," I said at last. "The Mexican bank won't allow me to cash a check in British pounds."

She reached into her Vuitton purse and got out some green. Money in any language.

"Here you go, Mr. Santana. That should be more than enough."

They were new 100-dollar bills, crisp as sandpaper, and some of them stuck together when I recounted them. Maybe she gave more than she intended. I said:

"Just in case I need to contact you, where're you staying?"

"The Hotel Francés," she replied. "Room 312."

Stubbing out the Delicado in an ashtray, I checked out her ass. Not bad. Just before closing the door she turned around and said, "Mr. Santana, I have your word that you'll leave this matter alone."

I gave her a stony stare. To tell you the truth, up to now I hadn't given two hoots in hell about Tristan's case. It was simply more money in the till.

Tristan Watts was now a medical student in Guadalajara. After his own feeble investigative efforts had stalled, he'd hired me to try to get to the bottom of his father's death thirty-some years ago in a village south of here.

John Watts had been an adventurer and a journalist, of a peculiarly gringo type, who goes native with a vengeance, the kind who's a magnet for trouble. He'd been on hand for the Guatemalan coup in 1954. In Cuba during the Revolution, he'd known Castro and Che Guevara personally. Watts wrote for the *Boston Globe* and helped cement the legend of Castro north of Key West. The charismatic, bearded young lawyer and revolutionary captivated the American public: he was Cuba's Robin Hood, David to Batista's Goliath, and newspaper readers couldn't get enough. After the Revolution, John met the British aristocrat, Lady Carolyn. They traveled to England and then Mexico, where their son Tristan was born. They were all living a hippie idyll on the banks of Lake Chapala in the summer of 1971, when Watts fell off the face of the earth. Two weeks later, a fisherman casting his net found his bloated corpse floating in the lake.

Before, I hadn't thought there was much more here than a rich brat's gnawing curiosity about how dad had died. After Lady Watts' visit, I was intrigued.

Instead of eating lunch, I walked to the coroner's office, just around the corner from the Viejo Hospital Civil. The clacking of a mechanical typewriter filled the office. If Don Horacio was in a good mood, he'd give me some crumbs of information.

"So you're still in the same job, Santana," he said. The coroner's calm brown eyes gazed at me. Fifty years of butchery, poisonings, and murder hadn't dimmed their childlike gleam.

"I see you're still at the same job, too," I commented.

"I could never retire. I'm afraid I might become one of my customers." He gestured to a glass case full of brass bullet casings and a row of smiling skulls. "What can I do for you today, Mr. Santana?"

"I just came to say hello."

"You've got something," Don Horacio regarded me brightly. "You are like the Americans, Mr. Santana, when you get friendly I know you're up to something."

"That so. Well come to think of it, there is something," I said. "Could you look up something for me? An American who drowned in Lake Chapala. His name was John Watts."

"When did this happen?"

I braced myself for the coroner's wrath and blurted out, "July 1971."

Don Horacio pressed his lips together under his bushy white mustache and grunted. After a moment, he called his secretary on the intercom and asked for the file. The clack-clack-clack of the typing ceased.

I lit up a Delicado. Don Horacio didn't mind. That's what I like about Mexico—you can smoke anywhere you damn please.

Two cigarettes later, Don Horacio's secretary came and deposited a coffee-stained folder in front of him. Shortly thereafter the typing resumed. Don Horacio opened the folder, looked it over, sniffed and grunted.

"Drowned," Don Horacio confirmed.

"Any unusual details?"

"Contusions on the back of the skull."

"Could that indicate foul play?"

"This could have occurred before he died or when he fell off the pier. A number of things could have happened aside from foul play."

I made a mental note to myself to ask Lady Carolyn if her husband knew how to swim, and said, "How long had he been in the water?"

"A week to ten days."

"Was Ministerio Público advised?"

"No, there was no reason to pursue it . . . Cause of death was drowning."

"Thank you, Don Horacio," I shook his smooth, pale hand. "Thank you very much."

Afterward, time for a break, so I walked downtown and parked myself at my table in the Café Madrid, got my cigarette lit and opened today's paper to see if I'd won the lottery.

"Mr. Thantana," a spit-soaked voice slurred at my side. "Juth the man I want to shee."

The slurred voice belonged to an old man in a wheelchair. Half of his lips were pink and rosy, the right side, bloodless, drooped like a helicopter shot down over 'Nam. His left eye was on fire, his right, dull, dead, a lost wandering child under a half-closed lid. I first met Grayson Hills while on the Heller case—a devil's broth of greed, murder, and gringo retirees. Until his stroke, Grayson wrote for a little real-estate rag that caters to gringo retirees, so we were on the phone every week, and they sold a lot of papers. At the Café Madrid, Grayson wheeled himself in close, close enough to feel the mist of spittle that came out every time he uttered an 's' or 't.' He had lived too long in Mexico to cut straight to the chase, and beat graciously around the bush, asking about my mother's health and pet goldfish and sour stomach. I turned my head to avoid the assault of projectiles.

"There's a mythtery at St. Matthew's Boo Glub," Grayson droned on, his words, once uttered in a crisp baritone, now scarred humiliatingly by slurps, lisps, wheezes: *wash* meant *was*, *Boo Glub* meant *book club*. "I wash on vacation, and when I came back one of the club's ledgers had dithappeared. It was in a logged box and I wash the only person who knew the combinathon . . ."

I tried to follow him and tasted my Delicado. Not bad for fifty cents a pack.

"Our glub was founded many years ago by a gentleman who headed the CIA mission in Saigon. He set it up sho everyone is assigned a five-digit number, and when members of the glub check out books, they use their numbers. Never their names. This level of shecrecy may sheem ludicrouth." (Ludicrous was definitely a word which Grayson should no longer have been attempting.) "But shome members, pasht and preshent, have ties to the agency and prefer the added shecrecy."

"What's the problem? A list of books and numbers."

"I wish it were as shimple. You shee, our founder

wash an informathon junkie. He left a code boog, that crosh-indexed all the names and numbers. It's a practice other glub librarians have followed. We have all the ledgers, ash a matter of fact, but th7e code boog is missing. And it goes back to when shome men were agtive agents."

"And you want me to find the code book?"

"If it's poshible . . ."

"Maybe you can sell a lot of newspapers."

"This won't be any Heller case," Grayson said, slurring and spitting. "This is gonfidenshal even to members of the glub . . . You don't have to tell them about the code boog or anything elsh. They don't know it exists. Just loog and lishen—you know when to shut up. You a good man, Tony."

"See what I can do," I said, humoring him.

"What will you want fum me?" he asked, reaching shakily for his pocket.

"Nothing. I know you, Grayson." He insisted like the gentleman he was and unfolded a purple 500-peso bill. "No, I can't," I told him. "I really can't accept that. Put your wallet away."

Tell most Americans that, and they put their wallet away. Grayson reached inside and handed me a few more hundred-peso bills.

After going to the Café Madrid, I strolled back to my office. I took Lady Carolyn's crisp 100-dollar bills in one hand, peeled off one for myself, stuck it under my desk calendar, pocketed the rest, and put on my leather jacket and headed across the Plaza de Armas and toward her hotel. My conscience, if you can call it that, started to twinge. No way I was going to drop Tristan's case, and I had to tell Lady Carolyn. It's easy to have a conscience when your wallet is full.

Carolyn answered the door, eyes red-rimmed, and a glass tumbler in one hand. It contained pale amber liquid. Even more fascinating was what her other hand held. A Glock semiautomatic, a nice little number made of lightweight plastic and easy enough to get through Mexican airport security.

"Oh, it's you," she said and untensed. "You can't be too careful in this country . . . There's a lot of violence in Mexico."

"No doubt, you know from past experience," I said, shutting the tall, carved door behind me.

A bottle on the nightstand was half full. The angle of the lamp shone across her shapely legs and ankles, tanned and waxed.

"I thought you and José Cuervo were divorced," I remarked.

"There's been a reconciliation."

Gently I took the gun from her and made sure the safety was on and gently put it in the nightstand drawer.

"I came to give you a refund," I said. "I can't accept it. Because I'm still going to follow through on Tristan's case . . ."

"This is precisely what I paid you *not* to do," anger in her voice. "Respect my peace of mind."

"Your peace of mind is driving Tristan crazy. If you hadn't been so secretive all these years, maybe he wouldn't give a rat's ass what happened to his father."

She stared morosely off into space. Then she remembered the drink in her hands and took a sip. She shuddered a little at the taste, and I knew she wasn't a regular lush.

"I want to ask you one thing," I said. "Did John know how to swim?"

"Heavens yes. He was a very good swimmer. A very good swimmer indeed. He played water polo in prep school, won prizes, and in Ajijic he used to go down to the lake every afternoon after writing."

"You know you'd make a fine murder suspect yourself."

"Don't be silly," she said in her creamy English voice. "Who's talking about murder?"

"Well, you said John was a good swimmer. How did he drown in three feet of Lake Chapala?"

She lowered her face, averted her eyes. She then sobbed. The heavy sobs racked her body, her lips blubbered. I pushed a box of kleenex across the night stand.

"There, there. S'all right." She cried and I put my hand just north of her breast. "There, there."

I patted her shoulder and a flood of memories came rushing back.

The cobbled street they lived on in Ajijic and the summer rain streamed down it, leaving the smooth round rocks silver-shiny and a cilantro-smell pealed like church bells in the brisk air after the rains stopped and the sun peeked out from ominous clouds. Memories of how she redecorated the cottage with love-flowers pasted on the walls, painted day-glo colors, electric blue and saffron yellow, how she worked at Mrs. Willoughby's folk art store on the square and John worked on his book, his own first-hand account of the Cuban Revolution.

"Of course the book wasn't going so well. The baby was bawling all the time, and John had to take care of Tristan when I was at Mrs. Willoughby's, so he had a difficult time of it . . . We had a guest, a nasty man. A friend of John's from Yale. John was out pushing a stroller one day and meets this chap at a café on the square. This fellow said, I think I know you, and John thought surely this chap was mistaken because he looked so unlike anyone he had ever known. He had straight long hair and John Lennon spectacles. Then they turned out to be dear, old friends from Yale."

"You remember his name?"

"It was Brooks something. He had the same last name as that pipe-smoking American admiral."

"MacArthur."

"No, the one mixed up in Iran-Contra . . . Poindexter," she snapped her long fingers. "Yes, that's it!" She became astonishingly alive when she hit then name, blue flame flickered in her faded denim eyes. "Now the queer thing about Brooks Poindexter was this: in college he had been so square, John had introduced him to pot and Charlie Parker. By the time

Brooks came to Mexico, the flaxen hair fell to his shoulders, and he was a bigger hippie than John. John was the square now, reading Bible instead of Marx. John invited Brooks to stay at our house, even though it was cramped, to say the least. They laughed and chattered about Allende till dawn and smoked grass. I didn't really get to enjoy it, since I had the baby to nurse and rose early to work at Mrs. Willoughby's. It was fine at first, but this fellow overstayed his welcome. John accused me of being square and selfish. It *is* a great annoyance to have a young child and a husband, and deal with a houseguest. All at the same time. One night Tristan was crying non-stop, and I was desperately trying to sleep. I had to open for Mrs. Willoughby in the morning. Finally, I barged into the living room, screaming. A bizarre scene met my eyes. John and Brooks were playing a drinking game with shot glasses, Russian Haircut, it was called. Brooks had lost and John was shearing his locks with my pinking shears, for God's sake. I gave John an ultimatum: offer to pay him a night at a hotel or I was going back to England. After my outburst, his friend packed and left. His retreat was so sudden it made me feel somewhat regretful that I had been so harsh on him. A couple weeks later we got a postcard from Chile."

I looked at the fall of light across her cheek, the pale, sifted light made her wrinkles vanish.

"Whatever happened to Brooks Poindexter?" I asked Carolyn, paying more attention to the curve of her neck than the question.

"Never saw him again. He sent me a nice letter after the death of John. I seem to recall it was postmarked Miami. Years later I heard from someone he died of AIDS."

"You know you're really beautiful," I said and kissed her on the lips before she could say, "What?" and we sank into each other's arms.

Next morning I roused myself at the ungodly hour of 8 a.m. I kissed Carolyn goodbye, pulled the bedsheet under her chin, and headed to a meeting of the St. Matthew's Men's Book Club. I had to at least *look* like I was doing something for Grayson Hills.

In a side room at the Episcopal church, where the meeting was held, the old boys sat around goose-necked lamps and wingback chairs in need of new upholstery. The room contained the smell of stale coffee in styrofoam cups and long uneven shelves of books, and silence. There was lots of that. In the chess-playing silence I could hear the sound of individual pages turning and of arteries hardening.

Grayson wheeled himself over and introduced me to the group. "This is Tony Shantana," he slurred. The pale patrician gathering looked at me as if I'd peed in their morning coffee. What was he doing here, this goddamn Mex? Grayson explained to them I was the private investigator who helped him report on the Heller case.

"Grayson invited me to check out your detective

fiction," I said. "I wanted check out some so I know how I'm supposed to talk."

They chuckled and looked more like human beings. They could have passed for a group of Rotarians from Omaha. Just some kindly looking geezers who been involved in garden-variety coups and assassinations.

When the meeting had adjourned, I asked Grayson to open the strongbox for me. He closed a book with a cobalt cover and white letters that spelled *The Reckoning*, and wheeled over to a battleship-gray box kept under a pile of musty, yellowed papers. He looked at the combination padlock with his one fiery, sharp eye, scratched his head, and said, "Shoot!" He went to another shelf and looked in a notebook and mouthed numbers to himself. He wheeled back. Grayson did seem to be getting forgetful.

He twirled the dial a few times and opened the lid of the shiny, gray metal box. Inside were several black-and-white student composition books crammed with five-digit numbers and book titles, written in a neat hand.

"Everything's here exshept the code boog," Grayson said in a low voice.

I flipped through them casually. Nothing to write home about, not that I could see, and I handed them back to Grayson.

"You know," he said, "the combinathon wouldn't worg after I god back from Puerto Vallarta."

"Sure you didn't just forget the combination?"

He fixed his fiery eye on me. "I had the logsmith

come and cud the padlock off. I'm juth getting used to the new combinathon. I have to loog it up every time."

I thanked Grayson for his time and left St. Matthew's church and the old men in dim chess-playing silence, the silence of old age where God could checkmate you any time.

A little more awake, I had to apologize to Dulcinea, my burgundy Ford LTD, and drove her to the west side. Four-lane avenues and jumbo stores. The city fathers went whole hog for U.S. junk food restaurants, car dealerships amok with pennants, and loud billboards, and the better-heeled denizens of Guadalajara fell for it. They paid twice the price for a Big Mac in a country where the average laborer scraped by on five dollars a day. Whenever I was in this part of the city, I panicked that I left my green card at home.

Costco and Sam's Club had a fairly good selection of strongboxes, including the American Eagle model I'd seen at St. Matthew's. Proudly made in Singapore, the stickers said. The strongbox at the book club was a little too shiny, a little too unscathed. I figured whoever robbed the club's code book had taken the original strongbox, pried the thing open, and substituted a brand-new one.

My suspect was American and amateur. No pro would have done it that clumsy way. And Americans buy everything with credit cards, so I got on the phone with a friend of mine at the credit central in Mexico

City. All the credit charges made in this country have to go through this one office.

I knew somebody with a little pull there. Diana owed me a favor, anyhow, after getting her son out of a scrape with the Guadalajara police. I got her on the line. "Diana, darling," I said after all the usual crap about her children and grandchildren, "I want a report on all the credit purchases in the last month of strongboxes in Guadalajara."

I soon had in my hands a list of buyers of American Eagle strongboxes. Carmen Montoya Valdés, Carlos Rodríguez Soto, and Tristan Watts. Tristan Watts?! I called him first.

"Yes . . . Tony," he answered the phone a little groggily but on on the first ring.

"Tristan, I want to ask you something. Have you ever been to the St. Matthew's Book Club?"

"Yeah . . . why?" His voice trembled.

"It seems they're missing some important papers, and they'd like them returned."

"You're not, like, going to arrest me, are you?"

I licked my chops.

"No, I'm not, like, going to arrest you, Tristan," I said. "If there's a way to return the papers without anything being said, it can all be very quiet and discreet. Nobody has to make a big fuss. I would just like to know why you swiped the ledger."

There was a long pause, and I thought maybe he'd hung up. Grayson Hills was right. I knew when to shut up when other people, uneasy with their own silence, would have already been Hello? Hello? Hello? Knowing to shut up is one of my gifts, maybe my only gift. Finally Tristan spoke:

"Among my father's possessions was a copy of a book stamped 'St. Matthew's Book Club.' I've always kept it with me, always, through all my travels in Europe and Asia. *The Doors of Perception*. It's all I've got of him. I went to the book club asking if any of them had ever heard of John Watts, but nobody goes back that far . . . I wanted some trace of my father, anything, some trace that he had been alive."

Now I began to comprehend what his mother had meant when she spoke of Tristan's obsession about his father. He was a little off the deep end.

Before hanging up, I asked him to bring me the book-club ledger in the morning.

I dreamed of a giant lottery that night, where the numbers chased me across an emerald-green field. Then I came to the shimmering blue ocean and a toothless hag laughed. Her laughter turned into the grating ring of the old rotary.

While blinking sleep out of my eyes, I had to hold the receiver a few inches from my ear. The only words I could make out from the sorrowful, high-pitched wailing were "Tristan" and "accident." It was Lady Carolyn's voice.

She calmed down just enough to say, meet me at the Viejo Hospital Civil. I jumped into yesterday's pants and plastered my hair, what's left of it, onto my forehead. I drove Dulcinea, my immaculate LTD, to Calle Hospital and threaded my way through a herd of straw-hatted men and shawled women mobbed around the entrance, bereaved and confused. After bumping against a dozen shoulders, I asked for Tristan Watts at the reception. A nurse rudely pointed me upstairs, to the new wing—intensive care.

His mother stood on one side of the bed, sleepless and puffy-eyed. An artificial breathing machine whoosh-whooshed. Tristan lay there, eyes closed, a plastic tube shoved down his throat. His skin was pale and lifeless as paraffin.

"They found him on a street downtown," said a doctor. "Apparently a hit and run. He's very critical. He goes into surgery in fifteen minutes."

Before the doctor left, I asked him if I could see Tristan's clothes and possessions.

"I'm so afraid, Tony," said Carolyn. "This is deja vú . . . First my husband dead, now my son. I should never have come to Mexico. Never, never, never. It's a jinxed country for me."

"Don't worry. He'll be all right," I said, like a fool.

By and by, a nurse brought a black plastic Hefty bag. Inside, Tristan's shirt and jeans were unbloodied, but torn where the ambulance attendants had sheared them off. I checked the pockets: keys, some tissue bus receipts, a spiral notepad and a Trojan. It had been there a long time, long enough to wear the tiny print off the package.

"Why're you looking in Tristan's things?" Carolyn asked me.

"I'm looking for some papers."

"What sort of papers?"

"Nothing you'd know about. He was supposed to bring them to me this afternoon."

"Tony," she looked at me with eyes the color of faded denim. "I think I may have them . . . I found some things in his backpack along with John's clippings and albums tied up with his mania about his father. His grades were slipping. And I thought it might help to take away the material."

"Well, you sure picked a doozy of a time to help in this way," I said.

She looked downward and said, "I've had it here all the time. In my handbag."

She took out an album of yellow clippings and a student's composition book, full of numbers and book titles. I grabbed both, thanked Carolyn with a kiss, and left the hospital.

As I drove Dulcinea back down Avenida Alcalde, night was falling. The feria for the Virgin of Guadalupe was full swing in front of the Santuario church. People were already gathering around the *buñuelo* stands and carnival rides. Sooty-faced *mozos*, the fiendish gleam of born firebugs in their eyes, stood around the base of the towering fireworks, *castillos*, ready to be ignited after the final mass in honor of the virgin.

I went back to my office and called Grayson Hills to tell him I'd recovered the ledger.

"I didn't expect results so shoon, Tony. You're good," he wheezed. "Can you gum by my apartment– 5C, the Norman Apartments."

"When?"

"Tonight."

The material was on my desk and this was my chance to look. I read couple of Watts' dispatches from Cuba. He really captured it, the sights and sounds of the Sierra Maestra, the camaraderie of fighters fighting for their impossible dream. I felt as if I were there, crawling on my stomach over pampas grass, about to make the final march on Havana.

I opened the book club ledger and ran my eye down each page. On one dog-eared page appeared:

Checked Out	Returned	
39453	_The Teachings of Don Juan_, Castañeda, C.	
5/21/71	6/14/71	
39453	_The Doors of Perception_, Huxley, A.	
6/14/71		

Something struck me. From what Carolyn had told me, John Watts was becoming less of a hippie at the time of his death. These books seemed more like another man's cup of psychedelic tea. I also saw that, after a 15-year lapse, #39453 started checking out books again. My gaze slid down the list, jumping from military history to wu wu mysticism, with an occasional gossipy bio thrown in. Most recently, _The Reckoning_, Halberstam D. The cigarette dropped from my lips the moment I read the title of the book I'd seen in Grayson Hills' gnarled hands.

Christ. What if Poindexter (a.k.a. Grayson Hills) had played me for a hunting dog? What if hiring me to find the missing code book was a ploy to lead him to whoever was snooping around his espionage past? If Tristan died on the operating table, I would be an accessory to a fresh murder.

I called the intensive care ward and hoped to God Carolyn was there. She was.

"I think I've located Brooks Poindexter," I said, trying to play it down. "Alive and living in Guadalajara."

I gave her the address for the Norman Apartments on Avenida Juárez.

"Tristan's book didn't belong to your husband but Poindexter," I told her. "He probably left it behind when he was your houseguest."

"Tony, this is all a bit much for me," she understated like a true Brit. "I can't go, Tony. I can't. Tristan is still in surgery."

"Come with me, Carolyn. I want you there to identify Poindexter. See you in half an hour."

It took me about fifteen minutes to reach the Norman Apartments on foot. I stood there dumbly watching the traffic whiz by, my legs warmed against the night chill by exhaust fumes belching from the speed demons that raced up Avenida Juárez. I waited another twenty minutes, or so, as a tide of night washed over the city, and gave it up. I pressed 5C on the intercom, a garbled voice answered almost immediately. An angry buzz followed. I tugged open the heavy ornate iron grillwork door.

The tiny elevator, just big enough for a wheelchair, rattled up to the fourth floor. I knocked on 5C.

After a few seconds the door opened a crack. I saw Grayson's snowy white head behind the chain. He still needed a haircut.

"Tony," he said and wheeled back to give me a wide berth.

The apartment was clean and uncluttered. The back balcony commanded a fine view of the north side of the city. It was a relief after riding up in the cramped elevator and threading my way through the Norman's dusky, dimly lit halls. The Ferris wheel from the *feria* rose against the night. People screamed raucous screams.

"You god the ledger?" he asked, dispensing with the niceties.

"Right here in my jacket," I patted my bomber jacket. "Have you ever heard of Tristan Watts?"

"Who?" he asked, a geyser of spit reaching my hand.

"A young man who lies dying in the Hospital Civil."

He slowly opened his mouth, a thick strand of spit joined his upper and lower lips. His congested face worked, no words came out.

"I think you've been in Latin America too long, and you've picked up the bad along with the good. Who did you pay to do your dirty work, Grayson? The hackneyed ploy of running political enemies off the road, Grayson . . . or are you Brooks Poindexter?" I said, pushing my luck. There was no stopping me—when I talked to Grayson I saw the Kong guy who grenaded me. "What I recovered doesn't look like a code book to me," I said, leveling my gaze at him. "Tell me the truth. There never was a code book, linking the names of club members to numbers. Only a list of books and numbers. No self-respecting member of a spy organization would leave something incriminating like that. It was a ploy to get me on the trail. But you were concerned, all the same, that the ledger had fallen into the wrong hands."

A weak knock came on the door. Grayson looked blank, paralyzed.

"Sit back," I said with a stiletto twist in my voice. "I'll answer it."

Lady Carolyn took two steps into the room. She glanced at me. Her face was a broken mirror and I feared the worst—Tristan had died on the operating table. Then her sun-bleached eyes focused on Grayson. Her face acquired the cautious expression of someone on a lonely street sizing up a passing stranger under a streetlight.

"John?" she said tentatively.

"Carolyn . . ."

"How can you be alive?"

She hugged him to herself hard, his snowy head to her stomach.

"You're dead, you're dead, you're dead . . ."

"Only half dead . . ."

"John . . . is it really you?" "

". . . That thummer in Ajijic I killed Books Poindexter," he struggled with the flannel tongue in his mouth. His spindly arms contorted like a rag doll's. "It was shelf-defense. He'd been hired by a group of reagtionary Cubans to kill me. I didn't mean to push him off the pier. Really I didn't."

Seated in his wheelchair, the elderly John Watts gazed at us, unseeing. He seemed to behold Poindexter's body sinking from sight again, into a watery tomb.

"It was an agzident," he continued, "but the Mexican polish would never believe that. They'd log me up and throw away the key. They would eggstort my family. I had to dishappear for a while, Carolyn," he spoke to her and her alone. "The Cubans who'd hired him to kill me were pleased. The Agency heard shome good things, and they hired me ash a Latin American operative. Thash when I deshided go on being Books Poindexter."

Carolyn looked at him, taking all this in. She neither smiled nor frowned.

"Why did you do it, John?" she asked at last.

"For abenture, the hope for change. I always planned to gum back. I wrode you letters. Dozens. But it wash never the right letter." Carolyn sighed a forlorn sigh. "It shounds naive, but hope for a better world . . . As Books I shabotaged the agency from within. The bloody coup against Allende would have been bloodier.

The Contras could have won in Nicaragua. The CIA might have suksheeded in killing Castro . . . These were shings I did my part to peevent." His voice became tender, tender as a slurring paralytic can be. "Nobody knows about Books Poindexter any more. The Agency toog care of that," he opened his frail arms to her. "I'm here in the Shitty of Roses, retired. New life, new identity. You know whad they say, the only shin in espionage is getting caught."

"I just caught you, John," she said, a flatness creeping into her voice.

Her hand reached into her handbag and reemerged with the Glock pistol.

"You ruthless son of a bitch," she screeched. Her faded denim eyes blazed. "You ruthless, cold-hearted, ideological son of a bitch. You left me alone with an eighteen-month-old baby. And I loved you."

"I never stop loving you," he gasped.

She didn't look like she knew what she was doing with a gun in her hand, but she got off two rounds before I could block her. A thousand pieces of shattered mirror, the color of sky, fell to the floor. Grayson looked at her, slumping with a dime-size hole in his chest. He stayed face-down, eating the carpet. I leaned down and felt for a pulse.

It was nervous time, the time when children in the building would say: *That was a gunshot, mommy. No, I know what a gun sounds like, mijo. That was a firecracker.*

Then it happened. A crackling din of an attacking army burst my eardrums, the fireworks display honoring the Virgin rent the sky, spluttered and dazzled. The series of shrieking whistles and explosions honoring the Virgin of Guadalupe.

"Let's get out of here, Carolyn," I told her. I proceeded to knock down some books and harvested the dead man's wallet. Make it look like a robbery. Before leaving, I cleaned the doorknob with my jacket sleeve. I took the stairs, Carolyn got on the rickety elevator from another floor. Nobody had seen us come or go together.

Mourned by expats and Mexicans alike, Grayson Hills was buried in a little plot in the American section of Mezquitán cemetery. The Mexican press gave him a little item, "Gringo Shot in Robbery." The U.S. Consul decried violence against Americans, and that was that. Even the real-estate rag he had worked for stopped following the case after a couple weeks.

Tristan Watts's surgery was a success. The day after his father's funeral he was awake and talking. His mother gave him back the album of his father's yellowed newspaper clippings. She told him that his father had been killed by a man named Brooks Poindexter, and that Poindexter was long since dead. I felt no need to contradict her.

"Your father would be so proud of you, Tristan," she said, eyes tearing. "You're going to be a doctor. You're going to help people."

I saw Lady Carolyn one last time before she went to the airport.

"I'm still puzzled by one thing," I told her. "Why did you want me to drop the case?"

"I wanted to protect John and protect his reputation . . . It doesn't really matter now. Nothing does . . . The irony of all this is something John confessed to me before he died . . . the first time, if you will. When he was in Cuba, during the Revolution, he spent the whole time in the Havana Hilton, drinking daiquiris and cribbing dispatches from other reporters. The closest he ever got to Castro was standing in the throng of a victory parade in downtown Havana . . . They wanted to kill him for that, them and their damned paranoia."

A single tear flowed below the black oval of her sunglasses.

"It'll be all right," I tried to reassure her, knowing full well it never would be all right. Nothing ever is, once you've pulled a trigger on somebody you once loved

.

Credit

"Of course," Travers lied through his teeth. "Of course I have credit."

Travers falsely declared that he had a steady job and credit. Some unpleasant experiences in previous days had swiftly taught him what apartment managers were looking for. They wanted somebody with a job and credit, not somebody just off the plane and jobless— even though Travers' prospects were sterling. There was more mercy in a box of baking soda than in a building manager's heart.

How funny it all was. He was laughing his guts out, Travers was. He had come back to Los Angeles bringing Frida, his sparkling Mexican wife, with the intention of showing how easy, honest and efficient things were in the United States. Frida didn't come as a *mojada*, but with her green card, and the Travers had a well-nourished bank account to boot.

They returned the filled-out application and a deposit check to the lady manager of the Bermuda Arms, located on the fringes of Hollywood. She promised to call them the next day.

Mr. and Mrs. Travers waited confidently at the Sahara motel for the manager's reply. The phone never hummed or beeped. It never made a sound. They had to visit the manager in person and they went along the upstairs terrace to her Dutch door that opened on the top half. The manager, Juanita, always did business that way, her elbows leaning on the counter of the door's lower half, wearing a catty expression. Juanita was from Honduras or Guatemala or another of those postage-stamp sized countries. She jabbered in Spanish, mostly to Travers' wife with whom she'd struck up a friendship.

With a sad-clown face, Juanita recounted that the owner had rejected their application because Travers had no credit. The news was received by Frida and Travers with a desolate expression.

"But I've never had a credit card in my life," he insisted.

"And he's been out of the country for nine years," Frida broke in. "What does he want with a credit card?"

"The owner wants someone with credit," the plump manager said, returning Travers' uncashed deposit check. Seeing the sadness in their faces, Juanita said, in Spanish, "I have an idea. I like you people. I had a good *feeling* when I saw you." She used the word, feeling, in English. "Why don't you find somebody else to apply for you, someone who has credit. You know," she said, "when one door closes, God always opens another door."

The battle spirit was unleashed. An apartment at the Bermuda Arms was worth the fight. Aquamarine reflections from the swimming pool floated up between magnolia branches and fern-filled terraces, and there was a grill for steaks to sizzle on. It was a haven in the city to make you forget about the smog and the traffic and the smelly people camped out in the park across the street, and the price was right.

Next morning, Travers went down his phone list and left messages with six dear friends and a second cousin he'd met once or twice in his life. Five of the six had bad credit or no credit and were in the same boat. Without hope, he dialed his second cousin, whom he'd saved for last.

Blood must be thicker than water. The second cousin, Ethan, called Travers right back. Without hesitation, without an eyelash of protest, the second cousin agreed to be a stand-in renter.

Papers were signed, deposits were made. Ethan came to personally meet the manager. He was a jumpy young insurance man who worked in actuarial statistics. His colorless eyes looked at Travers and Frida with muted fear, and he stutteringly advised his kin to be very careful. Hollywood could be dangerous—just across the street was evidence: the raffish assortment of street people camped out in the park across from the Bermuda Arms—and he and Frida ought to avoid the streets after nightfall.

"In a neighborhood like this, your chances of being mugged are 13 in 100, and there is a one in 100,000 possibility that you could be murdered."

Ethan left Travers with these grim statistics and a low-wattage smile.

The next morning Juanita called the Travers in their motel. The owner had accepted cousin Ethan as a tenant; his credit was immaculate.

The Travers went on a victory trip that weekend to a lake in the mountains. It rained all weekend, but that didn't dampen their spirits.

On Monday they went back to the studio apartment and received keys from Juanita. Happilyh they moved in. It was home sweet home at last, and they turned the key and entered the door with a palpable sigh of relief. Right away Travers got on Juanita's phone and contracted electricity and had a telephone installed.

Frida Travers finally got to see American efficiency at work: the phone and lights were up within hours. In Mexico there had been cases where somebody had to die before a phone line became available.

At a street sale that same afternoon they got a table and chairs. Travers lugged the heavy oaken pieces up the stairs. Rivulets of sweat poured down his face and he was winded, but he and Frida were buoyed by the blissful sensation of outfitting a home, intensified by days of desperate apartment hunting that preceded this triumphal moment. Never had a meal been so delectable as the Chinese take-out the Travers enjoyed at the oak table that first night.

Later, the couple lay on the floor of their neat little new home, after making love in the venetian-blind-filtered twilight. They lay quietly in the growing darkness. Soon the quiet was broken by three knocks on the door—three sharp explosions in their ears.

"Big trouble," Juanita cried when Travers opened a crack.

His heart sank to his toes.

"It's your cousin," Juanita blurted. "He has called three times and says he can't go through with the deal."

"What!" Travers clasped his head in his hands. The room and windows warped around him. "Jesus Christ! That's crazy!"

"Tell you the truth, I'm a little wary of him," said Juanita. "Three times he called. He might even try to call the owner and it could cost me my job."

"You've got to help us," said Frida Travers from the floor. "You must."

Travers himself was too stunned to speak.

"Listen, I'll give you three days to find a new place," said Juanita. "You can sleep here and I'll keep showing out the apartment. OK?"

Travers called his cousin and tried to dissuade him of his treachery. As Travers pleaded with him, Ethan sputtered nervous phrases and actuarial tables.

"I'm doing this for your own good," Ethan said. "I was looking up the 90038 zip code. There is actually a one in 873,000 probability you could be murdered. There's a 63.9 percent chance it will be by gunfire, and the odds for stabbing . . . "

Nothing short of a soul transplant would convince the young insurance man to change his mind.

"I just can't go through with it. The liability," he begged. "You could burn down the apartment with a hot plate, or one of your guests could fall into the swimming pool and they'd sue me. Whatever happens, I'll be responsible. The apartment is in my name. I feel awful. This was all a big mistake."

"Your big mistake was having said yes," said Travers. "Now we've got the electricity and telephone put in. What are we gonna do?"

"Good luck," Ethan muttered weakly.

Apartment hunting again: studios with space for only one resident, decrepit places with threadbare carpets, the halls impregnated by old stale food smells, For Rent signs with numbers no one ever answered. And they spent the days wandering amid the strange poetry of street names like Avocado, Poinsettia, Rimpau, and Detroit, eyes burning from smog, every joint in the body enervated from sitting in the car, the gaze riveting on every neon-orange "For Rent" sign.

Dead tired, they came back to the Bermuda Arms that night. The manager Juanita was puttering around, watering hanging ferns on the upstairs terrace. She put down her watering can and whispered in hushed, hurried tones to Travers' wife. It came out that the owner was paying a visit tomorrow morning, at 9 a.m., to inspect the apartment and oversee a few final repairs.

At midnight Travers was lugging the heavy oak table down the stairs. It seemed twice as big and bulky as the day before, and he marveled how he'd ever gotten it up the stairs. The table and other pieces of furniture were accommodated in the garage that Juanita offered as temporary storage.

Finally, a couple blankets and pillows on the floor were all that remained of the Travers' furnishings. They soon fell asleep after the day's exertions and forgot to set the alarm. At five minutes before nine a.m., seized by panic, they folded the blankets up and hid them in a closet. They unplugged the telephone and hid it under the blanket. The roll of toilet paper was removed from the wall fixture and milk and Chinese leftovers were cleaned from the refrigerator. Frida even took pains to swab the water droplets from the porcelain sink—a sign of human habitation.

Again, they spent the whole day again looking at an unsavory array of apartments and coming back to the Bermuda Arms, exhausted and disillusioned. Fortunately, the owner did not visit on weekends, but Juanita had to show the apartment on Saturday and Sunday. Mr. and Mrs. Travers lay on the floor in their pajamas, still asleep, when the first prospective tenants tramped through the living room and kitchen to weigh the virtues of the shag carpeting and inspect the closet.

The Travers felt the nakedness of animals on display in a zoo. Juanita explained their presence, saying that Frida was her niece and she and her husband were spending a night on the floor after a trip to Las Vegas.

"People traipsing in and out as we're on the floor in our pajamas," Frida exclaimed. "This is a barbarity!"

"Welcome to the United States," was the only thing Travers could think to say.

Dead tired after another day of apartment safari, they trudged up the stairs and lay down on the carpeted floor. The knock on the door did not delay, a loud thumping of a fist on wood.

"Come to the telephone," Juanita whispered. "It's the police."

"Dios mío," exclaimed Travers' wife. "What could it be now?"

Travers said "hello" to the receiver of Juanita's office phone. In his ear he heard, "This is Detective Spiegalman, Los Angeles Police."

"Ye-es," replied Travers tentatively.

"What is your relationship to Ethan Crane? We found your name and this telephone number on a paper in his pocket."

"Yes, he's my second cousin."

"I'm sorry to be the bearer of bad news," said Detective Spiegelman. "Ethan was killed today in a liquor store hold up."

Travers came back inside the apartment and closed the door. "What happened?" Frida asked Travers, still speechless after the call.

"Ethan is dead," Travers said.

"Dead?"

"Shot in a robbery. I guess the actuarial statistics caught up with him."

Frida listened. Her face became glum. After a moment her glum face lit up.

"Maybe we could stay in the apartment," Frida said. "Juanita could tell the owner Ethan changed his mind."

"It's a risk," Travers said.

"If we don't risk, we don't have a chance."

"What if we get caught by the owner . . . ?"

"We will have to lie and invent," Frida said.

"Before, I thought it was only in Mexico where you had to lie and invent," Travers said.

"Welcome to the United States," said Frida.

Ethan Crane continued to have excellent credit throughout the following year. He was a model tenant who always paid his rent on time and caused not the slightest headache for his landlord.

It was living proof of what Juanita had once told the Travers, *When one door closes, God always opens another door.*

The Havana Brotherhood

Being a junior broker on Wall Street, Harry stressed to all his clients the need for thorough planning to achieve prosperity. So when it came to this caper, his very first, he'd planned it supremely well.

The knee-high stockings borrowed from Amanda, without her knowledge, were quite comfortable and easily concealed half a dozen black-market *lanceros*. According to Harry's original plan, another handful were jammed in the same inner jacket pocket as his passport. Sacrilege: an open provocation, to have the American eagle practically kissing the dynamite Cuban stogies rolled by Communist hands.

Harry also advised his investment clients to seize opportunity, even if it disrupted plans. And that's exactly what happened. Fate dangled a golden carrot in an overlit drug store in Puerto Vallarta. In addition to a dazzling array of pharmaceuticals, from codeine to Viagra, the drug store sold black-market Cohibas. They tasted good but drew poorly—the telltale mark of factory seconds. They went out frequently and had to be relit after only a few puffs. After Harry's third visit to the drug store, the acne-scarred clerk offered something exquisite in husky confidential tones.

"I know where you can get the real thing, amigo. I have a gift box a friend gave me after a visit to Cuba, and since I don't smoke myself . . ."

It was a dream to be devoutly wished by all members of the Havana brotherhood, that royal club of American smokers who smoked every good Cuban cigar they could get their hands on, nevermind the cost. Their motto "Cuban or nothing" drove them on an endless quest from the hearty Romeo y Julieta, to the robust Montecristo, and the flavorful H. Upmann to the pungent Hoyo de Monterrey. It was their holy grail, no less, and they stoically endured comparisons of "that thing in their mouth" to a certain part of the donkey's anatomy; dismayed their wives by crossing the Canadian border on the spur of the moment, extending their vacation two days, in hopes of finding a box of Sancho Panza squirreled away in the dusty corner of some dry-goods store, or they sprang a surprise weekend in Baja, ferreting out some rather pedestrian Flor de Canos (shredded filler) from the depressing heap of impostor Mexican Partagas and Montecristo.

In rapturous hour they would sit by a lighted fireplace in an opium reverie and puff nostalgia for old Havana, now forbidden as absinthe, and they would behold imaginary curls of hair and female contours in the volutes of receding smoke. To become a member in good standing of the Havana brotherhood one had to agree on but one thing: on the fine point of cigars, hedonism outweighed patriotism . . .

After more secret negotiations at the drug store and a furtive rendezvous by the *malecón* of Puerto Vallarta, Harry came into possession of a box of honest-to-God Cuban *lanceros*.

One problem remained: just how to bring them into the United States? He considered express mail, but what if they inspected the package? They would have his address, and he could expect a visit from Uncle Sam's agents. Harry could go overland on a bus, since border inspections were more lax, but this would mean canceling his flight and missing more days at the brokerage firm. Now aboard flight 913 Harry tried to ease back in his seat, but the annoying bulk in the small of his back was a constant reminder that this trip was unlike any other he'd ever embarked on . . .

Amanda, his on-again, off-again girlfriend for the last six years, wouldn't have the least inkling why he'd undertaken this risky mission. Being a member of the Havana brotherhood was a major factor, but really, his reason was, at bottom, nobler and frankly sentimental. He wanted an engagement ring for Amanda, a one-karat diamond encircled by emeralds. Stiff payments for student loans kept him forever behind the eight ball, now he needed a little extra cash to buy the ring. A stickler for preparedness, Harry had even gauged the ring size surreptitiously by adjusting a Romeo y Julieta cigar band to her finger playfully and seeing that the edge came up to the "V" in Havana on one side.

Amanda would be awestruck when she opened the tiny jeweler's box—"Oh Harry!" she'd exclaim, drawing it to her heart. Then she'd plant a big kiss on his lips.

A quarter of an hour ago—it felt like a century—he was among all the travelers sweltering in the Puerto Vallarta air terminal, queued up and waiting with their bulky carry-ons and fanning themselves frantically with tickets and boarding passes. A ring of greasy sweat oozed down Harry's forehead, matting his front hairs in damp tendrils, and the frigid wetness of perspiration gathered around his collar of Egyptian cotton. A Mexican woman in a faded dress caught his eye, and they both nodded in smiling assent. "Boy, it's hot," they shared the wordless thought as the woman's hand waved the heat from her temples. In New York, now, it was 28 degrees and snowing.

Nearby, a group of tanned, well-fed travelers bantered in heavily accented English. Probably some well-to-do Mexican-Americans who'd visited their homeland and shown off their American affluence to their poor kin south of the border. Harry scrupulously avoided eye-contact, fearing they might divine the unnatural squarish form lodged in the seat of his pants. Suddenly a plump woman from the group turned her head and spoke to Harry.

"Why don't you take off your jacket?" she said, her eyes full of suspicion. "You must be dying."

Before he could mumble out an answer to the nosey woman, the line moved forward and boarding began. Harry drew solace from a quick self-inspection: the bulky tweed sports jacket that had seen him through various Manhattan winters helped soften the boxy form about his hind quarters, and nobody would ever suspect that all the inside pockets were stuffed with contraband.

His solace was short-lived, though. Harry's treacherous mind remembered something he'd seen once in the *Times*. A young Colombian, who'd never broken a law in his life, risked smuggling cocaine into the United States, persuaded by the fabulous profits that could benefit his starving wife and family. In the course of his flight, the balloon packed with the precious snow concealed in his rectum had burst and the drug galloped through his veins. In the middle of another flight, a rings-of-Saturn, mind-blowing high caused by the released cocaine, the Colombian collapsed dead on the floor of the Miami airport, moments after breezing through customs.

Now Harry's jet had already left behind the patch of earthly stars comprising Puerto Vallarta and had leveled out in the darkening sky. He raised the sleeve of his oatmeal tweed jacket, already damp with mopped-up sweat, brought it to his forehead and its woolen fibers soaked up fresh drops. Opening up the air-conditioning ball above his head, Harry felt the air blow cool against his face.

On the other side of the aisle, a frazzled soccer mom addressed Christmas cards, although New Year's was already past. Dad snoozed. Sis was catatonic with earbuds. Little towhead brother was going loco trying to get a bright-painted Mexican top to land atop the wooden peg to which it was fastened by a string. Watching the boy's repeated failures, Harry grinned and forgot, if only for one sweet moment, about his pending crime. Two seats ahead, the plump Latino tourists sat in their loose tennis clothes sporting newly acquired tans. The Buddha head of the woman who'd spoken to him in the terminal rose above the headrest, and her eyes darted in prying nosey glances toward Harry. The woman turned to whisper an aside to her seatmate. Had the old witch detected something unusual in the seat of his pants? Would she suspect drugs and try to be a do-gooder and blow the whistle on Harry? The woman called over one of the stewardesses and Harry's heart beat faster.

Christ, thought Harry, they're gonna radio ahead to the airport and have a SWAT-team ready to surround the plane upon landing. Happy New Year!

What would he do if the stewardess came over and asked to see inside his pants? Harry was ready for this. He'd reply that he suffered steatopygia, the medical condition of overdeveloped buttocks. The stewardess would be abashed for having asked so indiscreet a question, and the nosey woman would shut up out of embarrassment.

His heart was beating faster and faster, and he started feeling a tiny sharp jab repeated in his chest. Just then a male stewardess returned with pillows for the traveling couples. Harry chuckled aloud over his unfounded fears, as he saw the flight attendant adjusting a pillow behind the woman's head with a maternal gesture.

Soon a bar car was being trundled down the aisle, bottles tinkling on top, and the stewardesses were reaching drinks over to the passengers. If only Harry could keep his mind on the stewardesses. Under ordinary circumstances they inspired a whole swarm of erotic fantasies—especially the older ones who with mascara, eye-liner, bulemia, and an endless flow of artificial smiles fended off the dragon of Old Age and Unemployment. The young fresh ones, so cocky, trim and arrogant lacked the tragic element necessary for true beauty. Harry's heart went out to the older ones, though it would be hard to explain their poignant appeal to Amanda.

Before the stewardesses reached Harry, he'd opted for a soft drink. Ordinarily he'd have a scotch and soda, but he wanted to keep a clear head. On the other hand, the key to a well-enacted crime was to behave as normally as possible. He had learned that from Dragnet and Columbo. But what all these televised crimes left out was the sweaty, nauseous tingling; the gnawing horror that seized the body and pit of the stomach.

When the blue-aproned stewardess reached Harry, he asked for a scotch and soda. He savored the first sip like the first glass of water after riding a camel through the Sahara. If there was a lesson to be gleaned from all this mental torture, what was it? Try to forget what doom hangs over us and seize the moment, live it up. Harry had let himself be annoyed by so many petty things in his non-criminal life: returning library books on time, not crossing a crosswalk on red, not littering and paying his taxes. Now, aboard the jet with a box of contraband on his ass, he felt something akin to a taste of real freedom.

Emboldened by the first sips of scotch and soda, Harry sought to open a conversation with the passengers beside him, in seats E and F. An elderly fellow with close-cropped silver-gray hair slightly balding at the temples had the window seat. His turkey neck and shirt were encircled by a huge necklace of dark wooden beads, big as Christmas-tree balls that hung down to his belly. Harry had seen the old geezer prance around Mismaloya beach every morning, drink in hand, his hide tanned to a nut-brown, setting off the white bristles on his sunken chest. He was always accompanied by a native girl a fraction of his age—she could have been his granddaughter. For days Harry had been unable to determine the relationship between the two.

Now the soft, unschooled child-woman eyed him from the seat in-between Harry and the old man. During most of the trip she kept her head on the old man's chest, her black eyes terrified, and her trembling hands clutched his shirt.

"You have some nice looking beads there, sir," Harry ventured.

"They are kukui beads from Hawaii," the man volunteered with a sly grin. "They're supposed to give you luck. And they gave me luck, all right. Look what I found in Porto Valarta," he gestured to the young woman. "That's my young bride Pilar. I'm Honest Bill O'Rourke, damn glad to meet you."

The old codger extended a knuckle-cracking handshake to Harry.

"Hello," Harry extended a hand to the young woman and her face reddened.

"Don't mind her," said Honest Bill. "She doesn't speak a lick of English. The poor girl is terrified. She's never been on an airplane in her life. She's the first person in her family who's done it."

"If she doesn't speak English, how do you understand each other?" Harry asked.

"Oh, we understand each other in bed," Honest Bill answered with a wink.

"Why do they call you Honest Bill?" Harry asked after a quick swallow of scotch.

"I'm a retired lawman, and I've got a pretty good reputation," said Honest Bill. "Tough but fair. I was police chief of Spokane, Washington for fourteen years and then became a widower," the old lawman talked on. His kindly drawl lulled Harry from the acrobatics of his palpitating heart, his manic rehearsals of the crime to be. "We were always going to travel, my wife and I. We postponed it 'til the kids had grown up and then decided to wait 'til after I retired. We had all the travel books, cruise ship brochures, *Foder's*, *Let's Go*, you name it," he said and his bleached blue eyes narrowed. "Two years ago Helen got the cancer. We had planned all our lives to travel together and by the time we got around to it, she was too sick. She could hardly talk at the end."

Honest Bill stared out the window at the moonlit expanse of fluffy clouds.

"I'm sorry," Harry said.

"I started traveling this year. Went to a couple of family reunions, one in West Virginia, another in Illinois, then went to Hawaii. The kukui beads gave me luck, all right. I found this lovely little lady on the beach in Porto Valarta and we got married."

She tugged on the black beads and sank her head more deeply into Bill's chest.

"Congratulations!" Harry said.

"Yup," said Honest Bill, "the little lady and I are off on our honeymoon. We're going to New York. I figger it's a good place to start showing Pilar my country, beginning with the Statue of Liberty."

"I'm going to New York too," said Harry. "That's where I live. Call me up and I'll show you the town."

He took out a business card and handed it to Honest Bill, and the two men shook hands. Something about this imagined tour of New York with Bill and Pilar soothed Harry's raw nerves.

Dinner—or a cardboard facsimile thereof—came and momentarily put an end to the conversation. Bravo, Harry! He congratulated himself for the wonderfully natural conversation sustained with the passengers at his side and in a flourish asked the stewardess for another scotch and soda. Harry fiddled with his dinner, peeling away the foil and opening a napkin in his lap, following the dictum to adhere to routine. In fact, his appetite had abandoned him; he couldn't have swallowed a pea, much less digest one. His stomach was tied up in knots and his body exuded a strange keen odor.

I'm dying inside, but nobody knows it.

He thought ahead to the outbreak of freedom, when he'd go past customs, mission accomplished, and take his first exhilarating steps down the passage to his connecting flight in Houston, a crushing weight taken from his shoulders. Free at last! It got Harry thinking about his job in the brokerage. His work in the cubicle was a legal form of enslavement that got him watching the clock and lusting after the brief gust of freedom that came at the end of each day, when he'd go out with Amanda or simply sink numbly into a chair in the apartment he shared with two Hindu brokers.

This isn't crime, Harry bravely told himself: *This is just another job. That's all it is. A job.*

The stewardess came and took away their dinner remains.

"Sir," she said to Harry, "you hardly touched yours."

"I wasn't very hungry." A hot blush burned his cheeks.

"Can I get you something else to drink?"

"Another scotch and soda."

The unidentified smell rose up through Harry's clothes and he suddenly realized what it was. It was so weird, almost synthetic, like something produced in a laboratory. The smell of fear. Halfway through his third scotch he realized his bladder wouldn't hold out much longer. After restoring his tray to the back of the seat in front, Harry rose and only the beaded smell of fear remained, an after-waft.

Cheeks aflame, he waddled to the lavatory, forced by his concealed bundle to assume a duck's posture and walk. The lavatory was occupied as he stood outside, desperate for its occupant to leave and troubled by his burning cheeks. If he didn't get that under control, his blush would wave a red flag to customs. Down the aisle advanced two flabby, tanned legs belonging to the woman who'd eyed him suspiciously in the terminal. If she got too nosey, he'd have to put her lights out and leave her sprawled unconscious in the lavatory.

Did I think that? Yeah, I did.

Reaching the area in front of the lavatories, the woman touched Harry on the shoulder and he felt the burning sensation spread from his cheeks all over his body. While Harry recovered, the woman spoke haltingly:

"Maybe you'll think I'm nosey, but I'm observant," she said in a low voice, "and I couldn't help seeing that square object in the back of your pants."

Harry was shivering, shriveling inside, and couldn't say anything. The two stared at each other for a mortifying moment, and Harry's lips started to tremble.

"Are you a terrorist?" she asked point-blank. Harry looked at her with the expression of a man pushed out of an airplane without a parachute, as she continued, "Do you have a bomb, and are you going to blow up the plane?"

Harry let out a sudden snort of laughter.

"No," he cried. "I'm carrying Cuban cigars in my pants. Here, I'll show you."

In the semidarkness of the rear cabin, he unfastened his belt, grabbed down inside his pants and took out the box of Cohibas that, thanks to the alchemy of smuggling, would turn into Amanda's engagement ring.

"I wanted to bring these back to the United States."

"I know all about it," said the woman. "We just came from Cuba ourselves. My husband along with my sister and brother-in-law were in La Habana, visiting family. New Year's is their big holiday, you know."

"You can travel there?" said Harry.

"We went via Mexico City," she said. "Where did you get the Cohibas?"

"In Puerto Vallarta."

"Well, let me tell you," she continued. "It's awful what people have to do to survive in Cuba. My brother works at one of the cigar factories and they pay off the guard so they can carry cigars out in their clothes. Or they have somebody keeping watch and from an upstairs window they throw the box to someone below. If they get caught selling cigars on the black market, they could go to jail for fifteen years."

"My God," Harry said, "I never realized . . ."

"You look at some cigars like that, and you never know how much suffering went into them. Excuse me," the Cuban woman said suddenly. "I've got to get back to my husband. He'll be relieved to know we don't have a terrorist aboard."

Harry was taken aback by the face that looked back at him, after washing his hands and splashing water on his forehead. Talking to the Cuban woman had soothed his nerves, and it showed. He looked serene, even bore traces of the can-do smile. The jabbing sensation in his chest had vanished. The cabin was dark when Harry left the lavatory several minutes later. He looked over at the Cubanos, the woman's head was drowsing on her husband's shoulder. When he sat down the box of cigars made a creaking sound. He looked to see if his seat companions took note. The young Mexican woman with the jet-black eyes was blissfully asleep, her head pillowed on the lap of her husband, Honest Bill, and his crinkly eyes were also closed.

Harry tried to sleep, but sleep was impossible. The visage of Baumgardner, his boss, entered his troubled mind—Baumgardner with the incredible arched eyebrow that shot halfway up his forehead when a deal folded or somebody sold at a loss. He enjoyed a good smoke indeed, but was one of these nouveau smokers, so Harry would give him one or two of the factory-second black-market Cohibas, and Baumgardner wouldn't tell the difference. Delighted and a little pompous, he'd show them off to friends at Third Avenue bars as he went through a whole box of matches trying to keep the thing lit. Nice practical joke—Harry smiled to himself.

All of a sudden he had a sinking feeling, not just due to the vertical fall of the airplane hitting turbulence, but something more. One crucial thing remained unsettled between him and his fiancée: his cigar smoking privileges. What an uneasy coalition existed between Harry, Amanda, and his cherished cigar.

The girls from Miss Porter's and the Swiss boarding schools never objected to his smoke; they even *enjoyed* the smell of a good cigar. It was a question of breeding. Amanda, on the other hand, always associated cigars with Uncle Sal from Brooklyn who chain-smoked Roi-Tans. To be sure, Amanda would put a damper on Harry's poker nights. The mere sight of a cigar, unopened in cellophane, elicited theatrical coughing fits.

He lowered the tray and started to write:

Dearest Amanda,

> *Let's get one thing out into the open.*
> *I want your hand in marriage and to share my life with yours, but for all to go well, let us smoke the peace pipe*

when it comes to my cigars. They've been a part of me since childhood, and will continue to be my boon companion.

Believe it or not, I smoked my first cigar when I was only four years old. After begging for weeks, Grandpa and I sat down in rocking chairs, me in the kid-size Hoppalong Cassidy mini-rocking chair. I was wearing Bermuda shorts, so the hot ash fell down and burnt my hairless legs. Served me right. That was to be the last of a good thing until my teen years. Since then, me and my cigar have been going steady.

Amanda, I love you more than anything in the world, and when you think of my stogie, don't just think of Uncle Sal and his cheap, filthy Roi-Tans, think of the man who loves you.

Please, please understand.

Love,

Harry

Harry read over what he'd written. It was legible despite occasional air-pocket bumps where the pen ran off the page, resembling the jagged course of the Dow Jones on a bad day. Afterward, he folded the letter up into his shirt pocket.

The long plane began to slope imperceptibly downward. In the cabin the glowing light to fasten seatbelts blinked on with a pleasant chime, which roused Honest Bill.

"Wake up, darling," Bill shook his child-bride, "We're already landing. See the lights."

She opened her eyes and later, with trepidation, approached the oval window to spy the dizzy night lights of Houston dipping and swirling and see, momentarily, the speeding cars on the beltway racing with the plane. In seconds, they would touch down with a squealing skid on the runway and an intercom voice would command the passengers to remain seated until the aircraft had come to a full stop.

Suddenly after two-and-a-half hours in the air, the jet had turned into the New York City subway at rush hour. Harry was standing and the plump Cubans stood to the front with their tennis whites, looking sporty and tired. Harry's heart thumped in gloomy anticipation of the next moments. Deceive Uncle Sam? Never. Harry Stockton was the kind of person who wouldn't jaywalk or misstate his income by so much as a penny. Yet here he was with contraband and guilt in his heart; why didn't God stop the crazy merry-go-round before Harry carried out his deceitful plan? Why didn't the fanatic leader of a fringe nation fire nuclear warheads and zap Houston before going through these next painful steps?

The airplane hatch opened and a stream of passengers deplaned. Honest Bill and Pilar, his seat companions, brought up the rear. In front he caught a final glance from the tanned Cuban woman, who raised a pair of crossed fingers in solidarity.

Don't think about it, Harry told himself, dear God, help me get through these numbing moments, so I can get the cigars through and scrape together enough to buy an engagement ring for Amanda. God, you know that we want to get married, please help join our two souls.

The deplaned passengers embarked on a series of shimmering, space-age air-conditioned tubes. Harry positioned himself sideways, fancying that it made his square buttocks less prominent as he slid down the mechanized runway. At least they were moving, going someplace. Seated back on the plane, he had been putrefying. The blond boy and girl were playing hide-and-seek around the stout legs of the Christmas card mom, laughing and giggling. The towhead boy stole a couple of strange glances at Harry.

"Mom," he said. "That man has a square butt."

The woman gazed at Harry, and his blood froze.

"A lot of people have things they can't help," she told the child. "It's not nice to stare."

Finally, the passengers of flight 913 poured into a gaping hall, a computer-age Ellis Island. Video-green signs directed Harry to a line for citizens only. This separated him from Honest Bill and Pilar, she wasn't a citizen. Harry felt naked and alone, even with the two Cuban couples directly in front of him, and from time to time the woman gave him a conspiratorial smile. Sweat was oozing from all his pores and a hot blush attacked his face again at the worst possible moment. Harry started wiggling his big toes to make the blush go away, and he prayed that nobody ask him to take off his jacket. At last the head of the line came and Harry was called to the passport counter. A gentleman of indeterminate race with a skull-like head smiled at Harry.

"Where did you go?" he asked with the precise diction of someone born outside the U.S.

"Puerto Vallarta," he answered, feeling the heat reach the roots of his hair. "A two-week vacation."

Why did he say that? Harry berated himself over the "two-week" detail. A readiness to supply too much information always brands an amateur criminal. The man with the skull-like head scrutinized Harry's passport and said at last:

"Ah, you have a nice tan." He handed back Harry's passport and added with a big gap-toothed smile, "Welcome back."

Harry had practiced walking back and forth in front of his hotel room mirror in Puerto Vallarta with the box of cigars inside his pants, bought purposely two sizes too big. The hidden cargo gave him a jutting belly and each step cost an effort. Now, after passing by the customs agent, he felt confident, almost jaunty, as he approached the last hurdle after picking up his suitcase from the carrousel. Soon he'd be hugging Amanda at JFK, enveloped in her smell of Chanel No. 5 and magazine-staffer sweat, cushioned by her warm flesh.

A young man who seemed dressed for the beach asked to see Harry's customs form. If not for the badge on his faded Lacoste shirt Harry would've taken the guy for another tourist. Meanwhile, a uniformed, heavy-set woman at the counter ahead was checking off Honest Bill and his wife.

"Where're you traveling from, sir?" the Lacoste agent asked.

"Puerto Vallarta. Down for a little breather," Harry mumbled.

"Where're you going?" the agent asked as Honest Bill and Pilar disappeared up a ramp to freedom.

"To New York. Home," Harry responded. *Home*— the word evoked a sudden plaintive chord.

The young man's ballpoint circled the blue seal of the U.S. Treasury Department on the form, and he scribbled some enigmatic letters to one side—R-S.

"Please go to the young woman over there," he signaled.

Harry wondered why he was going with her instead of with the frumpy woman who'd just checked off Honest Bill and Pilar.

"Where're you traveling from, sir?"

"New York," Harry snapped. "I mean I'm traveling from Puerto Vallarta *to* New York."

"Why are you going to New York?" she asked.

"I live there," Harry said, impatient.

"And you have nothing to declare," the agent gestured to his suitcase.

"Nothing . . . Oh yes, I bought some shampoo while I was in Mexico," he added for effect.

She asked what university he'd attended and his profession. Harry answered these questions truthfully. She asked him if he knew he was responsible for declaring all the things he had in his baggage and on his person. Trouble. So many times coming in and out of the country, customs had waved him on, never asked a question or laid a finger on his bags.

"Yes, I do," he said calmly, or so he thought, unaware of the sweat breaking out all over his body. He tried to make small talk about the weather in Houston as her nimble fingers went through his personal articles, comb, toothbrush and electric razor. Alien fingers touching his things seemed an awful violation. She even looked inside a bottle of shampoo, uncapped it, and peered inside.

The woman's honey blond hair was combed behind her ears and kept in place with a beret. Harry couldn't help noticing that she was pretty. Her fine nose reminded him of the daughters of his parents' Country Club friends, whom he had dated—that kind of girl, clean-scrubbed, and honest. That was the torture of it all, a pretty young woman instead of a hairy-chested brute with a gold tooth to do the dirty work.

A drop of sweat crossed his cheek and he decided to leave it there rather than call attention to it. Harry felt trapped in a devilish backwater, lonely and isolated, sharp and awake. He had to think of something to distract the agent. They should be flirting, two good-looking young people like themselves.

"What's your name?" he asked.

"Becky," she answered without looking up from the things she was examining. Becky's nimble fingers now worked through the clothes in Harry's suitcase.

"They're wet," she commented.

"It was, er, raining and I didn't have time to dry them."

"I don't suppose there're many washeterias in Puerto Vallarta."

An idea struck him. Come hell or high water, Harry didn't want to surrender the prize box of genuine Cohibas that would fetch 800 dollars in New York, or more. There was one last ace to play—the black-market Cohibas stuffed inside his jacket. If he would surrender those, maybe, just maybe, Becky would get off his case.

"Look, I'm going to miss my flight," Harry said testily. "OK here's what you want." He reached inside the tweed jacket, withdrew a handful of black-market Cohibas, and placed them firmly on the inspection counter. Sorry Baumgardner.

Becky looked at them and rolled one between her fingers. She looked at Harry steadily, but with sympathy. Harry felt he was winning the battle with Becky when she turned around and mouthed into a microphone, "R-S." How coyly they hid the iron maiden behind sterile acronyms. Shortly afterward, two uniformed men came to the inspection counter and asked Harry to accompany them. These official figures escorted Harry to a tiny room only a few steps away from the throngs of travelers entering the country without a hitch, and a white door shut behind them.

The closed door hid a world completely isolated in the midst of the bustling airport; here the agents could be beating out someone's brains or putting electrodes to their balls and no one would be any the wiser.

◆ ◆ ◆

"Ah, what have we here . . . ?" a young agent said facetiously as his expert hands detected the bulky wooden form in the seat of Harry's pants. He was spread-eagled against one wall of the relentlessly white room.

The Cohiba gift box was removed from Harry's rump and softly laid beside the other cigars already confiscated from inside Amanda's knee-high stockings. The sallow older agent opened the box and took a whiff. His young partner removed one cigar and rolled it between his fingers, fresh and spongy. He peered down one end as if he were lining up a pool cue.

"There's nothing more inside these?" he asked. "No drugs?"

Harry broke down. "Pure tobacco," he hiccuped through the sobs.

"Do you know that these are not permitted in the United States under the Trading with the Enemy Act?" The elder agent took over explaining, and his colorless eyes acquired a penetrating gleam. "There are some differences between our government and Cuba's. We don't see exactly eye to eye. They have a system that is called Communism, and by buying these cigars, you are aiding Communism. Do you understand?"

"Yes sir."

The younger fellow, a bit damp behind the ears, was awed that the cigars couldn't be brought into the country.

"He bought these in Mexico, not Cuba," he rallied to Harry's defense.

"Still it's Cuban merchandise, trading with the enemy through a third party."

Harry couldn't hold it in any longer and he asked, "What are you going to do to me?"

"It's all up to the I.A.," said the older man. "Here sign this. It's a paper saying we didn't rob money or anything else from you."

Only my dignity, Harry thought.

While Becky coldly reviewed documents and looked at Harry's passport, a paternal-looking man in a charcoal-colored sweatshirt approached the counter strewn with Harry's clothes and personal effects. "Son, it would have been better to carry them in a suitcase," he pronounced with sad humor. This was the I.A., the inspecting agent, who held Harry's fate in his hands.

Harry had dried his tears and replaced his keys and wallet in his pockets before being accompanied outside the little white room. Now, mustering all his courage, he asked the I.A., "What are you going to do?"

"Crossing international borders with contraband and trying to deceive federal agents and breaking the law of the land, this is a federal matter." The man in the sweatshirt let it sink in. "We're all grown-ups here, so you'll understand what I'm saying. Customs has got bigger fish to fry. Do not let this be a dry run. Son, we don't look kindly on this, and hiding it on your person and in ladies stockings shows criminal intent . . ." He bored Harry's head with a withering, bloodshot glare that made Harry's heart contract. "We have your name, Harry Stockton, on computer and from now on, wherever you go, whatever country you return from, you will be taken aside and bodily searched. Smuggling is smuggling."

"Yes sir."

"What do you do for a living, young man?"

"I'm I'm a s-stockbroker," Harry stammered.

"Look," said the man, "if I tried to do a stock deal, I'd look pretty amateurish, wouldn't I? You'll never know how many things give away a smuggler. If people only knew, they'd never try it."

Harry's nascent criminal pride was insulted.

"Do you know why I did it? Do you know?" Harry said, angry tears flashing in his eyes. "I wanted to buy an engagement ring for my girlfriend."

"Don't say? Ha. That's very touching, son," said the man, shaking his head. "I'd like to see what kind of engagement ring you can buy selling a box of cigars. Maybe you'd best start looking for that ring in Cracker Jack, son."

Suddenly little people, who gave the impression of belonging to a race of dwarves, carried out a garbage can. Becky, unsmiling, handed the agents the cigars, and they all pitched in breaking them in two, twisting and cruelly crushing them. In seconds they undid the beautiful work of man and nature, of seasons in the tropical sun, years of ripening in a warehouse, and finally the inherited skill of generations of master cigar makers who'd made these exquisite creations, and the long tobacco filler crumbled like autumn leaves into the receptacle. Breaking the cigars had the fascination of a bonfire in a forest glade, and all eyes were upon it. The black markets were strangled one by one and, finally, the gift box of Cohibas was opened, freeing a rich waft of their dark brown, earthy, aged bouquet, and Harry instinctively reached out to touch one, bring it to his nose, one last time, and whiff its glory. Why hadn't he simply smoked them when he had the chance? Why hadn't he proposed to Amanda? Now Becky pushed his hand away, a mild, yet oddly violent, gesture that banished him from his Havanas. Finally, the agents took the varnished cedar box itself, now emancipated and devoid of danger, and poised it to break over the can's metal rim.

"Maybe you should save that," the I.A. said to Becky with a dry chuckle. "Ha ha, use it for a paddle."

Becky finished filling out a paper with Harry Stockton's name, passport number, physical description and a description of the merchandise seized. Meanwhile, everyone smilingly watched as the garbage can swallowed the last broken glory of Havana.

"This document says that you, the importer, forfeit the merchandise you are trying to bring illegally into the country. Please, sign here," she looked up and handed him a pen. Her mouth remained frozen, a rictus of astonishment, and she looked from side to side with blue eyes as big as Texas.

"Where's Mr. Stockton?" she squealed.

Those who had been huddled around the trash can looked all around: Stockton had slipped away amid the mirth and confusion. He was sure a sneaky devil. "He's on the floor," exclaimed the heavy-set lady with customs.

Becky crossed to the other side of the counter and saw Harry passed out. She leaned down and clasped Harry's clammy hand in hers.

"Mr. Stockton, Mr. Stockton . . ."

Harry's eyes flickered open briefly. "Amanda," he whispered to the gauzy shadow inches above him. There was an extreme urgency to that whisper as he lay on the floor by the customs counter where he had collapsed.

"Amanda?"

"Yes," Becky lied, squeezing his cold hand. "Yes, dear." Becky stared at him, her blond head swiveled to the I.A. and fixed her terrified eyes on him . . .

More than a year had passed, now, since that debacle in the Houston airport. Harry's fiancée slowly drew the match up to the cigar, a wooden match of course, held gingerly between her tapered fingers. The ring finger showed off a diamond circled by small emeralds. After a series of short, strong puffs, the match flame flared and turned the tip of the cigar into a glowing disk, deep molten orange as the Mexican sun descending into the sea.

The quick reaction of a U.S. government employee had saved his skin. Harry felt alive as never before; his brush with the reaper had forever turned the page on a joyless craven existence. The first thing he did after being resuscitated was tell Baumgardner to take his cubicle and shove it. Baumgardner offered him a raise.

"I'm impressed, Stockton. You're finally showing some backbone. Something happened to you in Mexico. You're different."

Tomorrow Harry and his bride to be would exchange vows, vows they had penned themselves, as they basked in the presence of friends and family on Mismaloya Beach in Puerto Vallarta.

"So rich and mellow," effused Harry's bride, the newest member of the Havana Brotherhood, as they smoked together on the balcony of their hotel, a cool mist reaching them as the waves crashed against the rocks below. "The Cohiba definitely has a more resonant bouquet than the Punch. Subtler."

Unraveling yarns of milky smoke drifted out of her lovely mouth as she spoke, giving each word a sexual charge. Harry's soulmate now tasted her own freedom from loathed day slavery, and it gave her the chance to pursue her dream of a PhD in psychology, with a special emphasis in criminal psychology.

In his mind, Harry went back to the day in the airport when he'd been officially dead for three minutes, and Becky, the customs agent, gave him mouth to mouth that started both their hearts pumping. Harry gazed at her. Becky gazed at him. At the same time both tossed their cigars to the floor, stirring a flurry of sparks, and together they tumbled toward the bed for a heated preview of passions to come.

Photo by Don Goodman

A MESSAGE FROM GRAYDON MILLER

Warmest thanks for reading *The Havana Brotherhood*. I hope there was one story you really liked. That's enough for an author to reach happiness.

I invite you to tell a friend about my book and post a brief review on Amazon or Goodreads. Reviews are my lifeblood and help keep my humidor filled.

Cheers,

graydon

THE HOSTAGES OF VERACRUZ

"Graydon Miller writes like he means it."
— **Richard Lange**, author of *Angel Baby*

What is happening to the indigenous children in Veracruz? Nobody knows why they are disappearing, and nobody really cares. Then Peter Vandervoort, a foreigner living in Mexico, snaps a picture of the wrong person in the wrong place and stumbles into a nightmare. He alone will uncover the horrifying truth about what's happening to the children. When he meets a French journalist trying to salvage her career, it's hate at first sight. But each holds a piece of the puzzle that will save the children and ignite a passion as steamy as it is volatile.

Hostages of Veracruz, available on Amazon.

Fiction/978-1499545326

ABOUT THE AUTHOR

Graydon Miller, the Wizard of Fiction, grew up in Watsonville, California. He attended local schools and later went to Columbia University in New York. In 1983 he moved to Los Angeles to study cinema, but discovered literature instead. He lived in Mexico for nine years, where he enjoyed his first literary success with the publication of *Un invierno en el infierno* (A Winter in Hell). His other works include the organ-trafficking thriller, ***The Hostages of Veracruz*** (on Amazon) and a screenplay based on the notorious Black Widow murder case, which he covered as a reporter in Mexico. Graydon Miller lives in Hollywood.